Harlequin Romances

OTHER
Harlequin Romances
by DOROTHY CORK

Many of these titles are available at your local bookseller,
or through the Harlequin Reader Service.

For a free catalogue listing all available Harlequin Romances,
send your name and address to:

HARLEQUIN READER SERVICE,
M.P.O. Box 707, Niagara Falls, N.Y. 14302
Canadian address: Stratford, Ontario, Canada N5A 6W4

Dreamtime
at Big Sky

by

DOROTHY CORK

Harlequin Books

TORONTO • LONDON • NEW YORK • AMSTERDAM • SYDNEY • WINNIPEG

Original hardcover edition published in 1976
by Mills & Boon Limited

ISBN 0-373-02057-0

Harlequin edition published April 1977

Printed in U.S.A.

CHAPTER ONE

It was strange to be actually on her way back to Coolabah Creek, from where Jackson Brand had so unfeelingly banished her four years ago, Reya Barberton thought. 'So watch out, Jackson Brand—here I come!' she murmured below her breath half humorously. Only half, because she was really a little bit afraid of meeting him again—and of how he would react to her return.

The ship was slipping slowly, silently through the early morning sunshine into the blue waters of Sydney Harbour, and Reya stood by the rail on the promenade deck, nervy and expectant, a slim fair-faced girl with dark eyes and silky shoulder-length brown hair. Maura and Melinda Alford, the two girls she had accompanied out from England to join their parents in Australia, were in the dining room having breakfast and perfectly happy—thirteen-year-old Maura in particular, because they were with Warren Livingston-Lowe. Reya herself was too excited to eat breakfast, and besides, she didn't want to miss a moment of this regal progress up the harbour. Already she had picked out so many places she remembered—Watson's Bay and Vaucluse, Bradley's Head and Taronga Zoo Park, and there, somewhere in Pott's Point, must be the house where Warren's friends lived and where she would be staying for the next few nights. She wasn't sure if that was really a wise thing to do or not, but she had let herself be persuaded and had posted a letter to Aunt E. from Fremantle telling her a little deceitfully that she wanted to spend a day or two looking around old haunts before she arranged her plane flight to Djilla.

She hadn't mentioned Warren or his proposal, because she was rather doubtful of it. She liked him very much—in fact, she supposed the glamorous shipboard life had gone to

5

her head somewhat, for she had flirted with him shame-lessly in a way she hadn't known she was capable of. He was a television film director and cameraman who was re-joining his team in Australia where they planned to do a film on outback Queensland, part of which was to be shot on location, excitingly taking in the Wet. Reya had seen the last TV series he had worked on—a fascinating combination of documentary plus adventure story, with a love interest thrown in. Even Barry Alford, who said with a slight touch of highbrow contempt that there was 'something for every-one' in it, still switched over to that channel when the series was showing. It had been filmed partly in North Africa, and Warren had emerged from its creation with some tropical disease that had left him, months later, still enervated and in need of convalescence. Hence the long sea voyage to Aus-tralia instead of a brief air flight.

Now, as far as Reya could see, he was a hundred per cent fit and healthy, and before they reached Fremantle he had put it to Reya that he would like her to 'join the team' and provide the romantic interest in *South of the Gulf*. She was flattered but surprised, recalling the smooth and sexy girl, Berenice Esmond, who had played in the African film.

'*Me?*' she had said, laughing a little. 'But I'm not—I mean, Berenice Esmond was so—so polished and sophisti-cated—such a good actress——'

'Berry?' Warren had frowned slightly and a shadow had passed across his intelligent good-looking face. 'Sophistica-tion was on its way to spoiling her. Anyhow, she's gone on to what she thinks are better things,' he had said with a trace of bitterness. 'You're the sort of girl we need for *South of the Gulf*, Reya. I've known you quite long enough to make up my mind about that. You must meet Lucille and Arthur in Sydney, and Jon of course. You surely don't have to race off to the country immediately—you can spare the time to see if they don't confirm my opinion.'

He sounded terribly brisk and businesslike, and in her heart Reya was a little shocked. Had he been paying her all that very personal attention because he was interested in

6

her as a possible replacement for Berenice Esmond? She wondered briefly what were the 'better things' *Berry* had gone on to ... And here had she been, thinking she was enjoying a simple and uncomplicated shipboard romance—and loving every minute of it!

She had made one more protest. 'I'm not even an actress, Warren. I just don't know the first thing about it.'

'You'll learn.' She didn't know if he had said it carelessly or relentlessly. 'You have the brains and the potential—and the looks. Those great dark eyes of yours can express anything you want, and even when you hide them, that mobile mouth is well worth watching.'

So from Fremantle she had written to tell Aunt E. that she wouldn't be coming straight out to Coolabah Creek. Because what girl wouldn't be flattered and fascinated by a proposal like Warren's? Though she couldn't quite believe in it, never having had the slightest interest in becoming an actress, and she was quite sure that Arthur and Lucille and Jon, whoever they were, would quash the whole idea very quickly—and would probably, anyway, have some beautiful and accomplished girl all ready lined up.

Thinking about it now as she stood at the rail she grimaced slightly. She wouldn't be in the least surprised if the whole of this unlikely Cinderella story disappeared into thin air the moment the ship docked at the Overseas Terminal. She would be just an English girl handing over her charges to their parents and then going off to visit her aunt in the outback. That, till she had fallen in with Warren Livingston-Lowe, had been the whole point of her coming to Australia ...

Her heart gave a little nervous leap. They were so nearly there. There was Pinchgut, or, to give it its proper name, Fort Denison. She saw the harbour bridge, the gleaming sails of the Opera House, and she stared and stared at the city skyline, aware that it had altered very considerably since last she had seen it. She had been a schoolgirl then, almost seventeen years old, and moodily rebellious at being taken back to England after three years in Australia where her father, a constructional engineer, had been sent for a short term by his firm.

For Reya, mainly because she had spent spring vacations in the outback, Australia had become a mystic country, and its dreamtime had called to her compellingly. The thing was that, but for Jackson Brand's interference, she could have stayed on and lived at Coolabah Creek with Aunt E. and Uncle Tom. Her aunt had actually talked about it, and she was quite positive her stepmother, Hope, would have made no difficulties, even if her father might have needed a little persuasion. But that arrogant and rebarbative man from Big Sky had to put his oar in, with the result that Aunt E. reneged and said it was best for her to go with her family. It made Reya writhe still to remember how she had hero-worshipped Jackson Brand. Well, the last trace of hero-worship had well and truly vanished before she had left the outback for the last time. Though it had turned out to be not the last time, for now she was coming back, and when she met him again, which she was bound to do because he had always been a fairly constant visitor at her uncle's sheep station, she was certain she would feel nothing for him but dislike. Mixed up with that rather disconcerting little dash of fear . . .

The ship was drawing closer and closer to the wharf and the decks were crowded with excited passengers anxious to pick out the friends or relatives who had come to meet them. There would be no one to meet Reya, but the Alfords would be there to pick up Maura and Melinda and it would be pleasant to meet them again. They were nice people. She had worked for them for eighteen months after she took her diploma in housecraft. Hope had looked down her nose at Reya's modest ambitions and warned, 'You'll be pounced on by some family who'll use you and use you. You won't have any opportunity to make a good marriage—you'll become a "treasure".' Reya didn't know if she had quite attained that stage yet. At the Alfords', she had been virtually in charge of the housekeeping and the two children and she had been happy enough, though she had continued to dream secretly of returning to Australia and the outback—to the sunburnt heart of the country to which she felt in some mystic way she belonged—the paradise that had been snatched from her by the boss of Big Sky sheep station.

The strange thing was that it was solely because of her position as incipient treasure that she was now so nearly where she wanted to be. And solely because of that, too, that she had the opportunity of taking up an exciting career in television. Yet in her heart she half wished she had not let Warren persuade her to linger in Sydney. She couldn't really imagine herself replacing Berenice Esmond, and she was so keyed up just now that she wished she could get off the ship and go straight to the airport, catch a plane, and be at Coolabah Creek before nightfall.

She closed her eyes, discovering they were filled with tears. Oh, those days of swinging in the old hammock under the coolabah trees by the creek, with the spring sunshine so hot and the dusty scent of wattles hanging in the air! And early mornings in the big kitchen helping Aunt E. make bread—breakfasting at dawn and riding out on one of Uncle Tom's horses across the paddocks to see the lambs being tailed and marked. She recalled the gorgeous sunsets and the huge star-filled sky at night, and felt herself shiver with apprehensive delight. It was all going to happen again, though she had thought so often that it never would. Would it still be as wonderful as she imagined? Or would the reality be tawdry beside the dream?

Someone clutched her arm and Melinda's excited voice said, 'Reya! There's Mummy and Daddy! Oh, isn't it smashing? I can't wait to see our new house. I wish you were going to live with us again!'

Reya opened her eyes to smile down into the child's flushed face before she searched the crowds on the narrow balcony of the terminal building, and finally located the Alfords, waving and smiling. Further along the promenade deck, a girl of eighteen or so was jumping up and down and croaking out a raucous 'Mum—*Mum*!' and waving frantically and sounding more and more like a cockatoo, so that

9

Reya was amused as well as touched. It must be wonderful to be coming home. She wished that Aunt E. could have been there to meet *her*, but it was too far to come, and anyhow she was staying a few days in Sydney.

'Maura's walking round the deck with Warren,' Melinda offered after a moment, her voice and face wistful. 'She didn't want me around. She's fallen in love with him.'

Reya smiled faintly and thought of her two pretty blonde stepsisters that last spring at Coolabah Creek. Lesley then had been about thirteen, and Jean, Hope's other daughter by a previous marriage, sixteen—a few months younger than Reya. They had all imagined themselves in love with Jackson Brand, though Reya had never admitted to it, and they had all—Jean in particular—engaged in all sorts of tricks to enable them to see him on every possible occasion. It was embarrassing to remember the chance meetings that had not happened by chance at all, and the fact that she, Reya, had been so hopelessly involved. She hadn't helped Aunt E. nearly so much as usual that month, and even now—after four years—she felt her stomach turn over at the very threat of remembering how it had all ended.

'Don't think of it now,' she advised herself determinedly, and she told Melinda brightly, 'I'm going down to the cabin to pack up all the odds and ends. You keep your wits about you, and the moment you hear the announcement that we can go ashore, head for the gangway and watch out for me. We must go through Customs before you can join your parents, and you and Maura will have to find your luggage in the section marked A. For Alford,' she added in explanation. 'As I'm B., we should be able to stick together anyhow.'

Melinda made a rueful grimace. 'I wish Warren's name began with an A. I suppose we shan't see him again once we go ashore.'

'No. You'll have to say goodbye soon,' Reya agreed. She hadn't told the girls anything about Warren's proposition, nor the fact that she was to meet his business associates.

'So will you,' said Melinda.

'As a matter of fact, I shan't,' Reya admitted. 'I'm not going outback for a few days, and Warren has asked me to stay with some friends of his at Pott's Point.'

'Oh!' Melinda's blue eyes grew round. 'Do you think he wants you to marry him, Reya?'

'No, of course not,' Reya said, and meant it. She had never had any illusions about that, nice though Warren had been. 'Just because we've been good friends during the voyage it doesn't have to mean anything like that. So please, Melinda,' she concluded, 'be sensible. Life on a ship is a thing apart. The real business of living begins again when you go ashore.'

'Going to school,' said Melinda. 'I suppose the girls will call us Pommies.'

'Only in fun,' said Reya. 'I went to school in Sydney for three years. It was the same as in England.'

'Life,' she thought, turning away at last and making her way down to the cabin. 'It's like a wheel turning and turning, and the same things are always coming up again.' Maura was thirteen. What was ahead of her? But Maura didn't have a mother whose twin sister had married an Australian sheep farmer. 'We are all, after all,' she reminded herself, 'individuals. We all have to learn our own lessons.' But she hoped that Maura would never have to learn the lessons she had learned—at Jackson Brand's hands . . .

An hour later she was waiting in the Customs shed with the girls. Outside, and visible through the big windows, Margaret and Barry Alford waited. Further along the big hall in the L section, Warren had not yet even appeared. Reya was beginning to feel slightly nervy and rather alone. She began to feel a prickling fear. Perhaps she shouldn't have come. Yet she had had to. Fate simply didn't present you with an opportunity like this without any meaning. So what did it mean? That she was to return to Coolabah Creek—for ever? That she was to encounter Warren Livingston-Lowe and be introduced to a new career? She didn't know. Suddenly even the idea that she could be of any use to Aunt E. seemed like some excuse she had fabricated to insinuate herself back into what Jackson Brand so clearly regarded as *his* territory—so she could show him that she didn't after all have to take any notice of his likes and dislikes, his whims and his commands.

'Calm down,' she told herself, suddenly weary of thoughts that seemed to go round and round in her head like the wheel of fortune. 'Play it by ear.'

She heaved one of her suitcases on to the long bench for Customs examination and smiled at the official.

'Nothing to declare?' He smiled back at her in the friendliest possible manner. 'You're right, sweetheart. Off you go. I don't need to look at any of that lot.'

'And the children's luggage?'

He waved a hand. 'They're okay. No worries.'

Were Australians always as kind and easy-going as that? she wondered. She found a porter and had the luggage loaded on to a trolley. Margaret and Barry Alford were standing peering through the window and smiling broadly, and in a moment Reya and the two girls had followed their luggage out into the spring sunshine. Reya, over-excited, wondered if she should have left her suitcases inside, because she would have to wait for Warren. Well, it was done now, she thought, putting on sunglasses to protect her eyes from the brilliant light.

There was an excited reunion with the children's parents, Reya was greeted affectionately, and Barry exclaimed, 'You've been a treasure, Reya. We've really appreciated your doing this for us. We've found ourselves a beautiful home—you girls are going to love it,' he added. 'It's at Mosman with a view of the harbour, and you can walk down to Chinaman's Beach and take a swim any time you like.'

'All we need to make our lives complete is you, Reya,' Margaret said. By this time they had reached the Alfords' car, the porter was paid, and Barry began loading the luggage into the boot. 'After you've visited your aunt, you *will* come back to us, won't you? Of course if you must go home to England we'll pay your return fare, but we've discovered

12

we just can't live without you, you've been such a treasure.'

That word again! It gave Reya a chilly feeling. She didn't want to be a 'treasure'. She loved the girls, and she was fond of Margaret and Barry but—she was Reya Barberton, and she was back in Australia, and who knew what was going to happen to her? She might even become a TV star! Wouldn't *that* surprise the Alfords?

'We've found ourselves a housekeeper,' Margaret added. 'But she isn't you!'

'Anyhow,' said Barry, who had finished dealing with the luggage, 'you're coming along home with us now, aren't you?—to see our new quarters, so you'll have something tangible to think about when you're in the country. I hope you can spare us two or three nights.'

'She can't. She's going to stay with Warren,' said Melinda, turning from a swift appraisal of the Holden car.

Reya heard Maura's gasp of surprise followed by, 'Oh, Reya! You didn't tell me! Oh, you lucky thing! Mummy, Warren's the most smashing man—he's fearfully good-looking and he makes television films. You remember *Sand and Sunset?*'

'Good God,' Barry said. 'You mean Livingston-Lowe?' He looked hard at Reya, his eyes suddenly probing—almost prying, Reya thought uncomfortably, and the colour rushed to her cheeks as though she were guilty of something—of what, she didn't know. 'Now you girls shut up and let's get to the bottom of this.'

'You're not getting silly ideas about stepping into Berenice Esmond's shoes, just because you happen to bear her a slight physical resemblance, I hope,' Margaret put in, with a disapproving lift of her pretty eyebrows. 'She was Warren Livingston-Lowe's mistress, of course—and now she's moved up a rung of the ladder by running off to the States with some American producer. The way to the top for her would appear to be via the bedroom—so I really wouldn't recommend you to emulate her, my dear.'

They all looked at Reya, whose face had now gone pale. She didn't know any of the gossip about Berenice Esmond,

13

and she wished futilely that she hadn't told her plans to Melinda—or that Melinda had minded her own business. She said indistinctly, 'I don't know a thing about Berry Esmond's private life.' Then she stopped with a stubborn feeling that she just wasn't going to say another thing. It was none of their business that Warren believed she had acting potential. They didn't own her—she wasn't their treasure. And whatever she chose to do, no matter how crazy or unwise they might think it, was her own business. Completely.

'Well,' Margaret said after a minute, 'you simply can't go and stay with Warren Livingston-Lowe. You're just not *like* that, Reya. You're not the artificial over-sophisticated type. You're a sensible, reliable girl who's got her head screwed on the right way, and knows her limitations. A girl with decent morals——'

Old-fashioned morals, she meant, Reya knew. Morals such as a treasure should have. She didn't think the Alfords' friends were completely straitlaced, belonging as they did to academic circles where new moral concepts and campaigns for liberation often appeared to originate. As for herself, so far she had never been tempted to do anything her father, for instance, would disapprove of, and if she were ever tempted to stray from the straight and narrow path, she would—well, she would do what seemed right to her, she supposed. Her conscience was still operating!

She said coolly, 'If you believe that of me, Mrs Alford, then you shouldn't worry. At all events, I'm not going to *live* with Warren Livingston-Lowe in any sense of the word. I'm going to stay with friends of his for a few days, that's all. My aunt and uncle,' she concluded with much dignity and less truth, 'are aware of my plans, so you needn't feel responsible for me in any way.'

They were all staring at her—the girls with wonder and envy and speculation, their parents as if she had turned into some completely foreign creature. Then Barry said in a clipped voice, 'Well, so long as you're not getting any silly ideas about becoming a television star by getting yourself

14

linked up with Warren Livingston-Lowe——' He paused, but she said nothing, and he concluded, 'Anyhow, when all the excitement's over and life has settled down again and you've recovered from your brief encounter with a celebrity, then we definitely do want you to come back to your old job with us.'

'Yes, of course,' agreed Margaret, sounding relieved but still looking suspicious. 'After all, it was the whole idea behind having you bring the girls out.'

Reya sighed inwardly. Was she going to be made to feel a cheat if she didn't go back to them? They had known why she wanted to come to Australia. She had told them about her Aunt E., they had known she possibly might make her home at Coolabah Creek.

She said reasonably, 'I can't make any promises, but I'll keep in touch with you, of course.'

There was a tiny silence. 'Do that,' said Margaret stiffly, and obviously displeased. 'Let me have your address, will you—the country one, I mean.' She opened her handbag and produced an address book and handed it to Reya. Reya extracted the tiny ballpoint pen, found the B section, and a little reluctantly wrote the Westwoods' address. She had the feeling Margaret Alford might have plans for making quite sure her aunt did know what she was doing in Sydney.

As she handed back the book she said firmly, 'Now if you'll excuse me, I really should go and see if Warren's through Customs yet.'

She didn't wait to see them drive off, but after goodbyes had been said, and she had kissed the girls affectionately, she turned away to go back to the Customs building. She hadn't very much enjoyed that little scene with the Alfords. She felt vaguely upset, because she had liked them so much and been so happy working for them. Now it was somehow spoiled. She didn't know, either, whether or not she was being a fool in going to stay with Warren's associates. 'Well,' she thought, 'everyone makes mistakes, and if you never take even the slightest risk, then how do you learn anything about living or about yourself?'

Suddenly she felt desperately tired. She had been up late last night—Warren's fault, their last night on the ship—and then she hadn't been able to sleep because of her excitement about what was ahead of her. She had risen before five this morning, to dress and go up on deck and, most foolish thing of all, she hadn't had any breakfast. She paused in the shade of the building, feeling just slightly faint. She had left her luggage on the footpath and she didn't care tuppence what happened to it. She didn't imagine Warren would be through for a long while yet—he was probably still on board the ship. What she needed was a cup of coffee, and after a moment she went into the reception hall where there were tables and chairs and where one could obtain refreshments. She had put her sunglasses away and was carrying her coffee to an unoccupied table when something made her look up.

A man was standing a few feet away scrutinising her thoroughly from under dark eyebrows. A man with black curling hair and a thin-cheeked, strong-jawed face that was tanned to an incredible deepness. His eyes were so blue that they shocked, against that dark skin. For a second Reya thought she was going to pass out. The blood left her face and everything swam before her eyes. Her cup rattled against the saucer, and perspiration broke out on the palms of her hands. Her lips parted soundlessly.

Jackson Brand!

Looking tougher, darker, more disturbing than she remembered. She had imagined this meeting often, but it was nothing like she had dreamed it would be. The fear was there, and the dislike—oh yes, that too, she hated him! So what was different? And what was he doing here? He couldn't have come to meet *her*. That would be crazy beyond the realms of possibility, because Jackson Brand didn't want her anywhere in the outback. So *he* wouldn't be coming to welcome her, to take her home. He was more likely, she reflected wildly, here to tell her to stay away!

A long moment had passed, and then he said, 'Hello, Reya.' His voice was as she remembered, a slightly flat

16

drawl in it that was typically Australian. 'It *is* you, isn't it?
I saw you outside and couldn't make up my mind—four
years have made a difference! You've changed your hair
style, haven't you? And those great dark eyes of yours were
well and truly hidden behind your sunglasses.' He moved
closer and taking the shaking coffee cup from her hand, set
it down on the table.

Reya groped for a chair and sat down. She didn't know
what had happened to her. It wasn't merely weariness or
hunger. Some mad spasm of acute emotion that she couldn't
analyse had shot through her, leaving her heart hammering
and her legs weak. She raised her head and looked at him
again, her dark eyes half veiled by her lashes. His hair, his
rather high cheekbones, that enigmatic mouth that was
slightly crooked so that one couldn't always be sure if he
was smiling or not. He was the same yet—different, and
she didn't know how, because he still looked tough. 'Get out
of my country,' he'd said, that well remembered day when
he had flung her on the couch and kissed her. 'In future
don't romanticise either me or the outback—we're both
tough and hard and brutal and ugly and practically impossible to live with. Go back where you belong and forget us
both.' The words came back to her whether she wanted it or
not, and she held her breath in a kind of agony, so that it
wasn't until he had lowered his lean length into the chair
opposite her that she managed to utter a word.

'I didn't—I didn't expect to see *you* here,' she said,
gathering together all the composure she could muster.

'I suppose you didn't,' he agreed, studying her through
eyes as blue as jewels against the teak-dark of his face. 'But
here I am. I came to meet you. Watch that coffee,' he added,
mockingly. 'You're spilling half of it in the saucer.'

Reya took a gulp of coffee and pushed back her hair with
a hand that was still uncomfortably clammy.

'Why have you come to meet me?' Her voice sounded incredibly cool. 'To—to remind me that the whole of the outback belongs to you or something, and you don't want me
anywhere in it? Well, I don't care what you want. I'm not

interested in you or Big Sky, just in—just in my aunt and uncle and *their* property, so——' She stopped. She had got carried away and he was smiling crookedly.

'Don't get so worked up about it. I'm not asking questions about why you're intent on coming back. I can work that out for myself anyhow. You always had that fever in your eyes when you found yourself in our primitive surroundings.' His eyes flicked over her disconcertingly. 'But since you've mentioned it, as a matter of fact I *don't* think it a good idea for you to return to the haunts of your youth —just as it's not a good idea for an alcoholic to take a glass of whisky, and for much the same reason.'

She put her head up, her cheeks flaming. 'So you're going to tell me to stay away. Well, I'm sorry, but this time I'm not staying away, so it's just too bad if you've come all this way to put me off.'

'Don't fool yourself,' he said coolly. 'I haven't come all this way to tell you anything. I've been down south to see a property I've bought, and right now I have a plane to meet in'—he glanced at his watch—'in just one hour's time. You may remember Marlene Ramsey. She's due in from Western Australia on her way home.'

Marlene Ramsey! Reya's heart gave a disturbed leap. She remembered Marlene very well—the girl from Lilli-Pilli, a property near Coolabah Creek. The girl who had been going to marry Jackson Brand. Instead, for some reason, she had married a mining engineer from the west. Reya had seen her wedding photograph in a women's magazine shortly before she and her family went back to England. So she had jilted Jackson Brand, Reya thought—'no wonder, and serve him right!' Now she said, 'You mean Marlene *Newell*, don't you? Is—is her husband coming too?'

The blue eyes narrowed. He had lit a cigarette, drawn on it once and crushed it out almost absentmindedly in the heavy glass ash tray. Reya's mind went back sickeningly to the evening when she had snatched his cigarette from him and put it to her own lips—she, a girl not then seventeen. And he had said—— She cut off her thoughts abruptly as

18

Jackson told her briefly, 'Ted Newell was killed in an accident early this year.'

'Oh—I'm sorry,' she said inadequately, and now she couldn't stop her thoughts. He had come to meet Marlene, who was free again. Did that mean he was still in love with her? Was she coming because *he* had asked her? Why else? As she thought of it, something deep within her revolted at the idea of travelling to Djilla in a small plane in the company of Jackson and Marlene.

And then, as though waking from a dream, she realised she didn't have to, because she wasn't going to Djilla today.

She said, her voice shaking slightly, 'I'm not going to Coolabah Creek yet. I wrote Aunt E. that I was going to spend a day or two in Sydney.'

'I'm aware of that,' he said impatiently. 'But surely it can wait till you're on your way back. If you really must honour us with your presence—and personally I'd have advised you not to—then I suggest you come along with me now while it's convenient and save everyone a lot of trouble.'

Reya felt her anger rise at his tone and wondered how she had ever been naïve enough to admire a man so uncompromisingly disagreeable and undiplomatic. Had it not been for her brush with the Alfords, she might have burst out with the news about Warren. As it was, she wasn't going to give him the opportunity of making snide remarks about her possible dramatic expectations, and she merely said, 'I've made other arrangements. It doesn't suit me to come now.'

His brows lifted. 'You can alter your arrangements.'

'I don't want to. I'm waiting for someone.'

His glance sharpened. 'For whom?'

'Nobody you'd know,' she said smartly, and wondered as she said it if it was true, or if the name of Warren Livingston-Lowe was known even to outback people.

He looked at her for a long moment without speaking. Not steadily but thoroughly. Those shockingly blue eyes of his moved from the top of her head and her dark shoulder-length hair, lingered on her eyes, travelled to her mouth—

19

too wide, she knew, too mobile and expressive to allow her to hide much, as Warren had told her—then to what could be seen of her above the edge of the table. She was wearing a white woven cotton dress printed in red with the word LOVE, over and over, Warren's favourite dress in her rather limited wardrobe. Hers too until this moment, when it somehow seemed exhibitionist, ostentatious . . .

'And what then—when he comes?' Jackson asked finally, his voice icy cold.

She didn't contradict his use of the masculine pronoun, she merely said, her head up, 'That's my affair. When I'm ready to come to Coolabah Creek, I'll let Aunt E. know.'

'And someone will have to drive in to Djilla to meet you, whether it's convenient or not. I think you'd better quit making a damned nuisance of yourself and come along with me now.'

'I don't care what you think,' she said, her colour rising. 'Aunt E. won't mind coming to meet me.'

'It's a long hard drive,' he said unequivocally, 'and a totally unnecessary one, seeing I'm here and my car is waiting in Djilla at the airfield.'

Her eyes smouldered. 'I don't see why you have to come into it at all. My aunt or uncle always used to meet us when we were schoolchildren.'

'Agreed,' he said pleasantly. 'But those days are over. One would like to think you'd grown up a little since then and could be considerate of your own free will.'

Reya shrugged and didn't answer. She wished she could catch a glimpse of Warren's violet-coloured shirt through the glass doors, but unfortunately she couldn't. All the same, she pushed her chair back and got to her feet, and Jackson stood up too.

'My friend should be through Customs by now,' she said coldly. 'And *you'd* better go or you'll be late at the airport. You can forget about me. I shall arrange everything with my uncle and aunt—it always worked out quite well in the past without your interference,' she concluded, being deliberately rude. She saw his mouth set and anger burn in his eyes.

'It might be better if you abandoned the idea of inflicting yourself on us altogether,' he said briefly.

She tilted her head provocatively and her eyes flashed. 'Us? What I do doesn't concern you. You made it your business once, but as you've just suggested, I've grown up since then and I don't have to take it. I can—I can do as I please.'

They stared at each other with hostility, and once again his eyes flicked over her.

'You're still so green it's unreal,' he said unexpectedly. 'It amazes me that E. suggests you're going to be any use helping her with the wedding breakfast.'

Reya's nerves jumped and she blinked with shock. The wedding breakfast! Amazing the logic of the mind even when one is almost knocked out. So it was on again with Jackson and Marlene now that she was widowed! Yet—her mind floundered—what had E. to do with Jackson's wedding breakfast? She asked gropingly, 'Isn't the—the reception to be held at Marlene's home—at Lilli-Pilli?'

'Sure it's to be held at Lilli-Pilli,' he said. 'Elaine's merely organising the food—catering for a crowd like that is outside Trish Ramsey's scope.' He paused and regarded her curiously. 'E. impressed it on me that you've acquired some skill or other that makes you an asset when it comes to catering. Otherwise——' He shrugged.

Otherwise, she finished it silently, he'd have somehow persuaded E. that Reya Barberton was to obey the old Keep Out injunction. So wasn't it almost laughable that she should be arriving just in time to help celebrate Jackson Brand's wedding? Suddenly her throat was dry and she swallowed nervously and told him, ignoring the 'otherwise', 'I have a diploma in Housecraft.' She didn't think it necessary to add that though it hadn't included anything like catering for weddings, she still happened to be a very good cook. 'But I don't think I shall be at Coolabah Creek in time to help with the—the wedding.' To her annoyance her voice had begun to quaver. 'Besides, can't Trisha help my aunt?'

'Trish knows her own limitations,' he said flatly.

Reya had never met Trisha Ramsey. Jerry, Marlene's and Susan's father, had married her the last year the Barbertons were in Australia and Reya knew she was from Djilla, where her father ran a small business. She remembered her stepsister, thirteen-year-old Lesley, breathlessly bringing the information of Jackson's coming nuptials after a chance encounter with Marlene. She had told Jean and Reya, 'Marlene couldn't marry him before, she had to look after her father, but now he's got this Trisha, and Marlene says she's a hopeless townie and she can't stand her, and she's got to get out before she goes off her brain. She said she and Jackson have been sort of engaged for ages, anyhow.'

Reya had felt stricken, but she hadn't let the other two know. She had felt as if she could die, she had thought Jackson Brand so wonderful. Well, she had got over *that*. And now he was to marry Marlene after all. It was odd in a way. She couldn't see him as the forgiving kind—the kind who would take back a girl who had jilted him. Still, she had to admit that, unlike Trisha, Marlene would make the perfect grazier's wife. She could do everything—she could even shear a sheep . . .

She put her head up. 'Well, I'm sure Aunt E. will manage quite well. Anyhow, I'm sorry, but I really don't expect to make it to the wedding.'

'No?' Jackson looked at her quizzically, and she thought irrelevantly, 'I know now what's different about him—he's wearing a suit.' She had never seen him in a suit before. He had always been in narrow-legged trousers and an open-necked shirt, and as often as not a wide-brimmed hat had shaded his blue eyes. And yet there was about him still such an aura of toughness, despite the light-coloured city suit, the white shirt, the dashing blue and green tie. His hair, at any rate, brushing his collar, was not much tidier than it usually was. It was very curly hair, and Reya had often thought it must be impossible to keep it tidy. She had even, once or twice, she recalled uneasily, longed to brush it for him, and even now her eyes lingered on it of their own accord so that she had to drag them away hastily. Some things were best forgotten ...

He moved a little and remarked pleasantly, 'So you won't put yourself out—and your few days in Sydney are going to be rather more than that. I think, if we can get moving, I'd better meet this friend of yours. I should like to be able to assure your aunt that I've left you in good hands.' He closed his fingers tightly on her arm and she flinched, aware of his strength, his remembered unpredictability. 'What arrangements have you made? Are you going to a hotel with him?'

She pulled herself free of him. 'Of course not!' she protested angrily.

'Of course not? But isn't that exactly the sort of thing you girls do so casually these days? It's accepted all round, isn't it? There's no longer any need for pretence and subterfuge, or to protest that it's a platonic relationship——'

'It is,' she said fiercely, feeling her arm burning still where his fingers had gripped it. 'Warren has friends at Pott's Point. We're going there, it's all perfectly respectable.'

'You've checked on that?' he asked cynically, and she said, 'Yes,' not caring in the least that it was a lie.

He said unexpectedly, 'Your dress is eyecatching. Love—so insistent. Who are you wearing it for?'

'Not you,' she said instantly and rather unnecessarily.

'Naturally not. You didn't expect to see me, did you? So I conclude that Warren must be the lucky man.'

'He's a very nice man,' she said shortly. 'Aunt E. would —approve of him.' They went through the door into the sunlight and as Reya automatically put on her sunglasses, she caught sight of Warren with a feeling of relief. He stood waiting indolently, gracefully, unconcerned, and looking— yes, she supposed he looked slightly effete, in his violet-coloured Italian silk shirt and expensive off-white jeans. He too wore sunglasses, and his hair, golden brown and well groomed, came almost to his shoulders. He was smoking a clove-scented cigarette, a habit he had acquired somewhere

23

or other during his travels. Glancing at Jackson, Reya saw his nostrils dilate and was aware that he was not impressed. The contrast between the two men was marked. Jackson, the taller by a good four inches, was the epitome of—not the rough type of Australian, but of the man from outback who belonged to a race apart. Yet he gave the impression of being well in command of the situation and he carried a distinct air of superiority.

Reya introduced the two men with slight nervousness.

'Warren, this is Jackson Brand, a neighbour of my uncle's. He's in Sydney to meet someone and he thought I might like to travel back with them. Jackson, this is Warren Livingston-Lowe.' As she said the name she watched Jackson and decided that it wasn't a name that meant anything to him, and she wasn't surprised.

The two men shook hands briefly. Jackson's eyes narrowed and his long mouth curved in a conventional smile as he said, 'How do you do?' and Warren said, 'Hello! You're from the outback, I take it.'

'If you like to call it that,' said Jackson. 'You're from London, are you?'

Warren's eyebrows rose slightly. It was pretty obvious his name hadn't rung a bell with Jackson, and while Reya was thankful for it, no doubt Warren was not. 'I'm from Bucks, actually,' he said pleasantly.

Jackson nodded. 'I understand you've asked Reya to spend a few days with friends in Sydney before she comes home to us.'

Warren looked distinctly surprised. 'Yes, that's right.'

Reya too was surprised—and a little annoyed as well, because it sounded almost as if Jackson, by his use of the word 'us', was trying to make it sound as if she were, at least partly, in his charge. Which she quite definitely was not.

Warren looked at Reya and said quizzically, 'I thought your home was in England.'

'While she's in Australia, her home is at Coolabah Creek,' Jackson said crisply, before she could reply. He added for

24

Reya's benefit, 'By rights, you should come home today. However, I'll tell your aunt to expect you in a few short days. You're to help her with the wedding business. Is that understood? She's depending on you.'

Reya stared back at him, baffled. She wasn't going to argue with him in front of Warren, but if he thought she was meekly going to obey him, then he was wrong. She said with a cool off-handedness, 'Don't worry, I'll get in touch with my aunt and explain to her.' Now work that out, she thought triumphantly—and for a ghastly moment wondered if he was going to step in bodily and carry her off by force there and then—there was that kind of a look on his face.

But nothing so uncivilised happened. In fact, he merely glanced at his watch and then at Warren—whom she was quite certain he didn't like. She wondered what he would tell Aunt E., and whether he would say he'd left her in good hands! Well, she had clearly won this round, anyhow, and made it plain to him that his word wasn't law with *her*.

He said, 'Nice to have met you. I'll trust you to look after this girl.' Nothing at all to Reya, not even goodbye, and the next minute he was gone.

Warren looked at Reya quizzically. 'Are all outback men like that? Does he have any right to tell you what to do, or was he just trying it on?' He put his arm around her shoulders and they began to move on.

Reya didn't know what she answered. She was utterly limp and exhausted and her nerves were positively jumping. Everything was confused—everything was somehow spoiled. Her dream of returning to Coolabah Creek had receded and receded. She wished futilely that there could have been no complications—none of this business of Warren wanting her to take part in his film, no Jackson at the wharf with his talk of wedding breakfasts. Just—just the trip out to Djilla in the plane and everything the way it had been—the way she imagined it. It was, she supposed, trying to laugh at herself, rather a lot to expect. Meanwhile, she was determined to enjoy her stay in Sydney. And she hoped that by

25

the time she got to Coolabah Creek, Marlene and Jackson would be well and truly married and away on their honeymoon.

And she just wasn't going to think about it.

CHAPTER TWO

IT didn't, however, work out the way she hoped. Not by any means.

Warren's friends welcomed her warmly and she liked them, though they were far more sophisticated than the people she was used to mixing with, and very different from the Alfords, who were older and belonged to a different group. Arthur and Lucille—she never learned their surnames—were in their late twenties, lively, good-looking. They lived together, but they didn't believe in marriage. While Arthur and Warren were talking in the lounge of their flat, Lucille showed Reya to a large bedroom with windows looking out over rooftops and trees—a lavishly furnished room with a lush carpet and an enormous double bed. Seeing that bed, Reya had a sudden and sickening suspicion that she was expected to share it with Warren.

Oh, God! What was she going to do? Talk about stepping into Berenice Esmond's shoes! She wished and wished that she had been weak and let Jackson Brand carry her straight off outback ... Yet surely she must be wrong about this room. Surely she was jumping to conclusions, and there would be a third bedroom in the flat, where Warren would be sleeping.

There was not, however. Lucille had left her on her own to change and unpack and make herself at home, as she put it, when the door opened and in came Warren with his luggage. Reya had taken off her Love dress and was in panties and bra, and she could have died. She turned her back swiftly and grabbed at a short kimono and slipped into it. She was shaking and on the verge of tears and couldn't turn to face him.

He said, sounding faintly amused, 'I'm sorry about this, Reya. It would have looked better if there'd been twin beds.'

She heard the soft sound as he deposited his luggage on the carpeted floor, and then he came and kissed her lightly on the back of the neck. She thought wildly of how she had flirted with him on the boat—of how flattered she had been —of his extraordinary proposal that she should begin a completely new life and play a part in the film series he was about to make—and she cursed herself for a simple fool. She had been asking for this. Everything Jackson Brand had suspected, and more besides, was right. All this flashed through her mind as she twisted away from Warren and said tensely, 'Don't touch me! When you asked me here I—I thought it was just to meet your friends.'

'Now calm down, Reya,' he said. 'I'm not a monster. I didn't rape you on the ship, did I?' He sounded completely matter-of-fact and unruffled, and just a little tired, and curiously, she did calm down—enough to wipe her eyes and to listen. 'As far as I'm concerned, you're just here to meet my friends. I've already apologised for this set-up, but in my circles—well, when a guy brings a girl to stay it's taken for granted that the accommodation available will do—that there's no point in running around in circles setting up camp beds or whatever. But nothing's going to happen that you don't want. I'm not a bad case of sex starvation,' he concluded wryly.

He had moved away and she heard a click as he unlocked one of his suitcases. So he was unpacking, and what was she going to do about it? Even if nothing was going to happen, as he put it, the idea of sharing a room with him, or with any other man, simply didn't appeal to her in the slightest. And that bed! It was impossible! She wasn't nearly sophisticated enough to take that in her stride, even if Warren was. And undoubtedly he *was*.

She turned round, to find him imperturbably hanging his clothes in the big wardrobe. She asked shakily, 'Isn't there another bedroom? Couldn't you ask them—please——'

He looked at her quizzically. 'There's not another room, but don't get excited. I'm just an ordinary reasonable guy. Don't get me confused with that man you met up with on

28

the wharf this morning. He'd probably take what he wanted —he wouldn't spare you. I'm not like that. Still,' he added sounding bored, 'if you wish, ask Lucille if you can change places with Arthur. There's no need, but please yourself . . . I'll leave you to change now. You have a talk with Lucille and just don't worry.'

He was a nice man, she thought when he had gone. She didn't believe Berenice Esmond had been his mistress. That was just gossip—publicity. All the same, this was not the sort of thing she could accept without turning a hair. She knew it was true—as Jackson had said—that people lived together openly these days, but the idea didn't appeal to her, and she didn't even want Lucille and Arthur to think that she and Warren were on those sort of terms.

Yet, as the day passed, she simply didn't get round to talking to Lucille about her problem. There didn't seem to be an opportunity and quite ridiculously, she felt too embarrassed, which was absurd.

Lunch was late, and some theatrical people had been invited. The talk was of films and filming, of stage and television personalities, and Reya found it all quite fascinating though well outside her scope. One of the men present— Jon—had written part of the script for the Queensland series, *South of the Gulf*, and though Berenice Esmond's name was mentioned several times, nobody said a word about Warren's proposal that Reya should play a part in the film. Still, she was aware that Arthur was watching her, and it made her self-conscious in her gestures and responses, and nervous of talking. Not, she couldn't help thinking, healthy signs in a girl who would be expected to act a part.

'They'll all advise him against taking me on,' she told herself, and quite honestly she felt relief.

They all went out to dinner and met more theatre people, and by the time they came back to the flat Reya felt utterly exhausted. It had been a long and difficult day, and while the others were still talking animatedly and having a final drink in the lounge, she slipped away to her room. She still hadn't talked to Lucille and now it was too late. She would have to leave it to Warren. He would fix something up, respect her wishes, she assured herself as she crawled into bed and fell asleep almost instantly.

When she woke in the morning he was there, on the other side of the wide bed. Not touching her, but there. As though she had leprosy or something, she thought, and for a mad moment she wanted to giggle. And then she felt appalled. She scrambled quietly out of bed to shower and dress before he woke. It was very early, no one was around, and she shut herself into the lounge and phoned the air company, to arrange her flight to Djilla that day. She didn't know just when she'd made up her mind to do that, but somewhere along the line the decision had been made.

Then she put through a call to Coolabah Creek. It was a party line, serving three homesteads, and she wondered if the Ramseys at Lilli-Pilli, or Jackson Brand at Big Sky would pick up their receivers even though it was the Coolabah Creek ring. Just in case they did, she was careful what she said.

It was her aunt who took the call. 'Reya darling! How sweet of you to ring! Are you having a wonderful time with your friends in Sydney?'

'Lovely, Aunt E. But look, I'm—I'm homesick. I'm sorry about being such a nuisance, but will it be all right if I come on the plane today? I just can't wait to see you and Uncle Tom, and there's no flight tomorrow———'

There was a second's pause, then—'Of course, lovie. I'll tell Tom, and we'll be so looking forward to seeing you. I want to hear all about your friends in Sydney and—well, you know who———'

Before Reya could say any more, the pips sounded and as she didn't want to impose too much on Arthur, she said a hasty goodbye after promising to answer all E.'s questions when she saw her.

It was a relief to have it all settled before anyone else in the house was awake. She couldn't—she simply couldn't—

face another night in that bedroom with Warren.

She broke the news of her coming departure later on when they were all sitting round the dining room table drinking coffee and eating muesli and yoghurt, which was apparently the favoured breakfast.

'Healthy,' Lucille said. 'And easy to prepare.' She glanced over Reya's slim figure. 'You don't look like you eat much bacon and eggs anyhow—you're lots slimmer than Berry . . . Want to come shopping today? The men will be talking shop and Warren has ideas for changes in the script. Nothing that *we* can manipulate.'

Reya listened and reached for the bowl of yoghurt. It had been strange meeting Warren again this morning. She had felt embarrassed, but he had been completely unperturbed.

She said carefully, 'Thank you, but I can't come shopping. I have to go outback to visit my aunt and—well, I've been doing a bit of thinking, and—and I've booked on the flight today.'

Lucille stared at her in astonishment. 'Really? I thought you'd be here for several days.'

'I'm afraid not. You see, there's—there's a wedding coming up at a neighbouring station, and I have to help with the reception.' She stopped and spooned up some yoghurt nervously. They were all watching her, all listening to her, and she had a deep awareness that she didn't belong amongst them and never would.

Lucille said, 'Must you?' and Arthur said thoughtfully, 'Pity.'

Warren, for a fleeting instant, looked almost murderous, but he said nothing at all.

Later, when Lucille had gone shopping and Arthur was talking on the telephone, he asked her, 'Why? When you were so keen on the ship?'

Had she been so keen on the ship? She couldn't really remember. She said awkwardly, 'I really should have gone with Jackson yesterday. I—I can't stay, Warren. It would be no use anyhow. You know I haven't a clue about acting.'

'You'd learn,' he said. 'Your looks are all in your favour—

you're reasonably intelligent. You could be brilliant. You could be a find—a discovery. Things happen this way in my world—I've proved it. You could outdo Berry Esmond.' She didn't answer, and he continued determinedly, 'Cancel your flight—come on now, do as I ask, it's important to me, Reya. If it's this bedroom thing that's bugging you, it's easily remedied. We'll move out of here—go to a hotel, whatever you want. Just say the word and I'll go along with you. I can't have you walking out on me like this.'

She listened and felt more than a little flabbergasted. He surely couldn't have all that faith in her talent for acting— he had no proof of it whatsoever, unless his experience gave him some means of judging potential of which she was unaware.

'When did you book your flight?' he asked her curiously.

'This morning—early,' she answered stiffly. He was going to try to persuade her, but her mind was made up. The fact was, the mainstream of her life had been briefly diverted, but now it was time to return to it. Warren had been no more than an interlude. 'I could only have stayed a few days anyhow,' she added defensively. 'I do have to help my aunt with this wedding, you know.'

'I don't know, as a matter of fact. Whose wedding is it?'

'Jackson Brand's. The man you met yesterday.'

He smiled slightly. 'Well, that's something. I rather wondered if he had some sort of a claim on you, the way he was talking . . . All right then, go off to the wedding—do your duty, and then come back to us. Will you promise me that?'

She looked at him frowningly. It seemed that everyone was set on persuading her to do something different— something that *they* wanted. The Alfords, Jackson Brand, Warren Livingston-Lowe. But it was up to her to decide what she truly wanted to do, and that was, ultimately, to live in the outback. Yet perhaps she would be disillusioned after all this time. Perhaps she would discover that it's best to leave dreams, memories, alone. And perhaps it was largely obstinacy that made her want to return—a determination to prove something to Jackson Brand. She had heard Aunt E. say that if once the outback got into your blood, you couldn't ever leave it alone. It kept calling you back and back until finally it swallowed you up.

Reya didn't know for sure if the outback was in her blood or not, she only knew that all the while she was in England it had haunted her dreams. The red plains, the flat, flat horizons—the rider on the tall black horse who was, whether she wanted it or not, Jackson Brand. So she *had* to go back to find out. And once she had found out—then she would know whether she must make some other choice or not. Just now, she wasn't making any promises, and she told Warren firmly, 'I can't promise anything. My aunt may want me to stay. I just don't know when I shall come back to Sydney.' She nearly added, 'if ever', but she didn't. He looked definitely put out as it was.

'You won't be playing this silly game of now-you-have-me-now-you-don't in a few months' time, I promise you. I can't stop you going away, of course, but I'm not going to lose you just like that. I don't know just what's upset you, but don't be surprised if I follow you outback in a very short time. Once I've cleared up a few matters here, I shall quite certainly do that if you haven't come back to me first.'

Nothing further was said on the subject by either of them, but later that day, on the plane flying west, she thought of what he had said, and she found his determination baffling. She didn't think it was Reya Barberton the girl who interested him, yet she had neither the confidence nor the vanity to believe she could be a discovery—another Berry Esmond. However, her thoughts didn't stay with him for long. They returned instead to Coolabah Creek—to Big Sky—to the past. To all the memories she had kept so determinedly from rising completely to the surface of her mind lately. For now, with nostalgic and evocative glimpses of the country below and a stirring in her heart at this return to places once so well known, she could maintain her defences no longer. Her mind wandered where it would and eventually it took her back to that final spring.

'All right, remember it—remember every detail,' she told

herself with a kind of savage intensity. Even if she had to encounter Jackson Brand only at his own wedding, it was as well to keep the focus on the truth about him, and not allow herself to confuse him with what she loved. And so it was to Jackson Brand that her thoughts returned obsessively, and while the past was torture to remember, yet curiously it was pleasure as well, and while she lived it over she hated him, and hated all he had said and done, yet still held it to her. Well, he would be married soon, and that very fact must write *finis* to her memories and perhaps to her hatred.

It had been a traumatic spring, that last one, with her father's three-year term in Australia not many weeks from its end. Sixteen-year-old Jean, not in the least like Reya, but light-hearted, extrovert, had decided to fall in love with Jackson Brand—because, she said, she would never meet anyone in the least like him ever again, and it would be fascinating if she could discover how the boss of a big sheep station made love. Whether she had found out anything at all about that, Reya didn't know for sure, but she rather imagined she was the only one who had come out of it with any experience—she, whose thoughts had been secret, her feelings for Jackson unspoken, unadmitted to. Lesley, thirteen, had been an important pawn in the game. Jackson Brand, in the two preceding years, had been remote, almost godlike, and Reya had worshipped from afar, and been in awe of him whenever he came to the homestead to see Uncle Tom. She didn't know if it was her own growing maturity or Jean's example, but she too, that spring, fell hopelessly and secretly in love.

Her feelings, in fact, had got completely out of hand: she had been *sick* with love. She remembered now to the point of nausea the scent of wattle, the scent of orange blossoms and her own wildly romantic dreams in which Jackson Brand was hero and lover. Oh, the fantasies she had indulged in, she who had never been kissed except by one or two teenage schoolboys! Jean in her ardour persuaded Lesley to keep her ear to the ground, and wherever

Jackson Brand was going to be, there, if it was at all possible, was Jean too. And if Jean was there, Lesley and Reya were there as well, because Uncle Tom insisted they must stick together out riding. Lesley discovered which evenings Jackson would be visiting Coolabah Creek and which track he would be using. She knew which paddock he would be working and whether it was too far for them to ride out to. And if Uncle Tom was going to Big Sky, Lesley knew it and persuaded him to take her and Jean and Reya along too.

For the other two, it was a tremendous game, but it was more than that for Reya. She had always helped Aunt E. a lot in the homestead other years, but she very much neglected her duties that spring, she had fallen so deeply under the spell of Jackson Brand, the handsome, suntanned, virile boss of the biggest sheep station in the district, Big Sky—or to give it its proper name, Murna Morang.

She hadn't wanted to leave Australia—not only because of Jackson Brand, but because she adored the outback and because, for her, E. was truly family. He own mother and E. had been twin sisters. She didn't get on very well with her stepmother, Hope, and she had confided this to E., who had actually said she would like her to stay at Coolabah Creek. Then, quite suddenly, it was all off—simply because Jackson Brand, whom E. had inexplicably consulted, had advised against it.

'And of course he's right, darling,' E. said reasonably. 'It would be very wrong and very selfish to keep you here. Most girls would give their eye teeth to have the opportunities you're going to have when you go back to England. Holidays in Rome and Paris and Amsterdam—visits to galleries and theatres—*social* life ... Now I'm not going to discuss it, Reya, just take my word that it's best. As Jackson says, you'll have forgotten all about this part of the world in six months' time. You'll wonder why you ever wanted to imprison yourself here. It's not an exciting life, you know, lovey. In fact, it's often deadly dull and very lonely. And the summers—they're scorching, cruel.' E. was adamant. Nothing Reya could say, and not even tears, could move her.

And it was all because of Jackson Brand's interference. Reya couldn't believe it. Two days to go and he had killed her hopes. Why?

That same day, too, Lesley broke the news that Marlene Ramsey was to marry Jackson. It was the final blow, the end of everything. Reya's whole world disintegrated. To have to leave because he willed it, and to know that he was marrying someone else.

Now, as she leaned back in the seat of the aircraft high above the plains, Reya's skin prickled as she remembered what she had done next—and the consequences of it.

She had run down to the stables and asked Spence to saddle up Blackberry Tart for her, and she had ridden madly over to Big Sky with some illogical idea of making Jackson Brand put everything right. How, she hadn't even stopped to think.

It was late afternoon when she reached the homestead, but he wasn't there and she had sat in a cane chair on the wide green tiled verandah and waited for him. That year Everlie, who was the head stockman's wife and did the housekeeping for Jackson, was away in Djilla awaiting the birth of her third child, and there was no one about except a couple of aboriginal housegirls and, somewhere whistling around the yard, the cowboy. It was maybe an hour before Jackson came home, and he was furiously angry with Reya, just for being there. He asked what the hell she meant by coming to the homestead—and he accused her of chasing after him all spring.

'Every time I look up you're there, and now you're tracking me to my own house. What the devil do you want?'

'I want—I want to stay with Aunt E.,' she had stammered out, shocked by his attack.

'I've told E. you're not to stay,' he said freezingly. 'We've no use here for romantic little soft-shelled English girls. The outback would kill you in no time, if you had the sense to realise it—stone dead. We don't want you here.' His blue eyes stared down at her unreadably and her blood curdled at his tone as he towered over her. It was terrible to hear

36

someone you had idolised talking to you that way.

Tears stinging her eyes, she had jumped to her feet and given vent to her wounded feelings, her shattered dreams.

'Just because you're the boss of Big Sky, you think you're the centre of the universe—you think you own the whole of the western plains, that you can ordain who comes and who goes. Well, you can't—I'm going to stay with my aunt somehow, I don't care what you say!'

He gave her one level look, then took out cigarettes and lit up impassively. Without, she thought furiously, even offering the packet to her—as though she were a child.

Cheeks burning, determined to assert herself somehow, she demanded, 'I'd like a cigarette.'

'Well, you're not having one. Your Aunt E. wouldn't like it.'

And then—her cheeks burned at the memory of her childishness—she had reached out and snatched the lighted cigarette from between his fingers, put it to her lips, breathed in, choked and coughed. And Jackson Brand had said, staring at her through narrowed glittering eyes, 'That's a damned provocative thing to do.'

He had lit another cigarette for himself, but suddenly he had tossed it on the ground and crushed it out with his foot, muttering something she couldn't hear. The next moment he had seized hold of her and his lips were on her mouth. She never knew how it all happened, but she felt the cigarette she had snatched from him burn briefly against her breast as she was pinned beneath him on the cane couch with its cushioned overlay. She felt the weight of his body on hers and his fingers raking through her hair while his lips demanded something of her that had her petrified. She was held there for only a few seconds, and then, as suddenly as it had begun, it was over. He was standing at the verandah rail and she could hear him breathing hard.

He said, as she struggled to her feet, disturbed and shaken and roused in some bewildering way, 'Get out, Reya Barberton! I don't like girls of your kind. Get out of my country just as fast as you can. Stop romanticising, and know this—that the outback and I are two of a kind, tough and brutal and ugly and impossible to live with.' He hadn't turned round but had stayed with his back to her, and after a moment Reya had gone on shaking legs across the verandah and through the garden to where her horse was tethered beyond the fence. She didn't know how far she had ridden from the homestead, her thoughts almost suicidal so that she rode like a maniac, when suddenly there was another horse alongside Blackberry Tart and Jackson Brand's hand reached out and seized the reins and her horse stopped so abruptly that she almost flew out of the saddle. She fell forward over the pommel, sobbing silently.

If she had expected tender words or kindness, she was disappointed, and this was the difference between the real Jackson Brand and the man she had imagined him to be.

'Now pull yourself together and quit the dramatics,' he had said. 'You'll have forgotten all this in a year's time.' By 'all this', she didn't know if he meant what had just happened on his verandah or the whole of the outback. 'Girls like you and men like me should steer clear of each other. All we could ever be to one another is an experience—and not a nice one. You get back to your own civilised world where good manners and pretty conventions are laid on and there are no brutal battles. And just make sure the next man you have a crush on belongs in that world.'

'I haven't got a crush on you,' she had breathed out, controlling her tears.

'Then that's great, because you're no bush baby and I'm not a pleasant character, am I? ... Now are you going to ride back to Coolabah Creek sensibly or are you going to continue trying to kill yourself and your uncle's horse as well?'

She hadn't answered that, and he had given her one last long level look from his inscrutable, fiery blue eyes—a look that she had suffered again and again in her dreams—and then he had gone.

And she had never seen him again until yesterday.

She moved restlessly and looked down from the plane.

She didn't like him any more—she hated him. And she hoped that this time his marriage would come off and that he and Marlene would go away on a long, long honeymoon.

When she left the plane at Djilla, she wondered whether it would be Tom or E. who came to meet her. Maybe it would be both, she thought. The heat came up from the red earth and breathed its fire on her as she walked across the airstrip. From the air, she had noted absentmindedly that the country was green as if there had recently been abundant rain, and the air was hot. She had walked perhaps twenty yards, her head down, her sunglasses protecting her eyes, a small overnight bag clutched in one hand, when someone relieved her of her piece of luggage and Jackson Brand's voice said, 'I'll take care of that and see to your other gear. The car's over here.'

No greeting, no calling her by name, nothing. So Reya merely nodded and didn't even raise her eyes as she walked at his side, measuring her step to his long one, though she was a fairly small girl. She had worn, either rashly or defiantly, her Love dress and now she felt self-conscious about it. As she slid into the front seat of the station wagon she felt mild surprise that Marlene wasn't there, and she glanced up at Jackson and was struck anew by the dark tan of his skin that made his eyes look bright as sapphires. He used to be—and oh God, he still was—somehow larger than life, a presence, and of this she was afraid.

She asked, deliberately cool, 'Where's my aunt?'

'At the homestead. Where did you think? A totally unnecessary drive of a hundred odd kilometres is a little much to expect of her. And your uncle happens to have other things to do besides picking up wilful young relatives ... Have you got the receipts for your luggage?'

Feeling chastened and annoyed about it, she merely opened her handbag and handed over her receipts.

He was back in a few minutes, loaded her luggage into the car and got in beside her. As they moved off he asked disconcertingly, 'Why the sudden rush? What went wrong in Sydney?'

Reya flushed to the roots of her hair.

'Nothing,' she said casually, and turned her head deliberately aside to look out at the green paddocks they were passing as they drove fairly fast along the sealed road. This was the only quick part of the journey, for presently they would turn on to a gravel road, and after that they would be following wheel tracks. Her mind flicked back to other years when E. or Uncle Tom had picked up her and her stepsisters and taken them past Big Sky and home to Coolabah Creek on just such an evening as this, with the sun in their eyes and the tree shadows lying long and grotesque and dark across the pallor of the plains. She had never seen the country green as it was now. She knew it best strawcoloured with patches of bare red earth, and scattered over, as it still was, with blue bush and miljee.

As she looked, despite the unease aroused in her by the presence of Jackson Brand, her blood was singing in a mystic way as if she were coming back to her dreamtime, to that part of God's earth that called to her subconscious so constantly and so urgently.

She almost jumped when the man beside her spoke again.

'Nothing? I can't swallow that. Didn't you like Warren's friends? Or were the sleeping arrangements not to your liking?'

She bit her lip and the colour that had left her cheeks rose again. Quite certainly she was not going to tell him that she had had to share a room—and more—with Warren! She could just imagine the conclusions he would jump to—well, that anyone would jump to, she admitted to herself. She said nonchalantly, 'I just happened to find that one day in the city satisfied me after all. And I—I wanted to see Aunt E.,' she finished lamely.

'So it was sheer unadulterated eagerness to see your aunt that made you change your mind,' he remarked sceptically. 'If that's so, it's a pity you didn't get your priorities straightened out yesterday. It's a little ludicrous for anyone to have to waste half a day picking up one visitor, isn't it?'

Reya shrugged, although in her heart she agreed with

40

him. 'I'm sure if it was all that inconvenient for you my aunt would have come—or one of the men. You had some business that brought you to Djilla, I suppose, didn't you?'

'No, I did not. Quite simply, I was the one who had to pay the forfeit since I was the one who slipped up in not being sufficiently persuasive yesterday. Maybe I was hoping you'd decided to give Coolabah Creek a miss altogether,' Jackson added with a side glance in her direction.

'You don't have to keep pushing it,' she said. 'I know you don't want me around.'

They had reached the turn off from the main road, and as he swung the station wagon on to the gravel, he simultaneously flipped open the glove box and groped for cigarettes, steering one-handed. Reya watched fascinated as he extracted a cigarette from the packet, put it between his lips and lit up. She was disconcerted when he remarked, 'I hope you haven't by now added smoking to your bad habits since last we met.'

So he had forgotten nothing. Her pulse quickened nervously, and she didn't answer.

'By the way,' he said after a moment, 'I didn't ever get around to apologising for my bad behaviour that evening you invited yourself to my homestead.'

She quivered inwardly.

'I didn't expect you to apologise. I took it that it was the kind of thing you were used to doing.'

His eyebrows shot up. 'Really? I suppose that was a healthily basic mental reaction, however immature. But let me assure you that I'm not—and never was—as much of a rake as all that. You were little more than a child, though an extremely provocative one. Did you ever work it out that looking for trouble means more trouble? ... And by the way, you look scarcely a day older than you did then, despite the subtleties of eye-shadow and perfume.'

She moved a little away from him. She felt completely helpless in his company and quite unable to work out a satisfactory attitude to adopt. Most of what he said either puzzled her or, despite her dislike of him, stung, and she simply wasn't clever enough to work out a retort that would knock him out.

'Let's hope you have grown up, however,' he continued, 'and that a dash of disillusion has given you the beginnings of wisdom.'

'I get by,' she said, her tone dry. It was the best she could do and she didn't think it was too bad an effort. At least it earned her a surprised glance from his sharp blue eyes. She hadn't missed the point he was making, though. She had no doubt that what he had said was supposed to relate to her old obsession about staying in the outback. Well, she was here to investigate the validity of that, but it was strictly her own business.

'Schoolgirl crushes, I take it, are out,' he said half humorously. But if he was warning her, there was surely no need, seeing he would be married very shortly.

'Schoolgirl crushes were never in,' she told him brightly. 'I never did hold you in the—the esteem you seemed to think. You dreamed that one up yourself.' It was something she had imagined herself telling him, more than once—something she wished she had said that evening it all happened, but now his reaction was not the one she would have expected, for he laughed briefly and mirthlessly.

'Come off it, honey. You had an outsize crush on me—it was dripping out of your ears. You trailed me mercilessly the last time you were here—a skinny schoolkid with big black eyes, and you followed me round like a faithful hound. I couldn't move without bumping into you.'

'*And* my sisters,' she reminded him furiously. The blood was drumming in her ears. A skinny schoolkid! So that was how he had seen her! And now he had to humiliate her by telling her what he had thought! 'I *do* hate him,' she thought, and it was a deep relief. 'If you really want to know,' she continued, 'it was Jean who had the crush on you—goodness knows why. She was the one who—who wanted to follow you around. But it was only fun.'

'Ah yes, Jean,' he said reminiscently. 'Pretty and blonde and pert and obvious. What's become of her now?'

'She's private secretary to a lawyer in London.'

He nodded and drove on for a few minutes or so before he remarked lazily, 'But you were the one with the velvet, mysterious, changing eyes—the eyes of a child. And you were always there too, weren't you?'

'So was Lesley,' she asserted, her breath catching for some reason. 'Uncle Tom wouldn't let us ride about on our own.'

'Hmm. So where were the others that evening you rode over to Big Sky?' he wondered.

'You're too clever, aren't you?' she retorted. 'What are you trying to prove? You know why I had to see you that evening—you know you'd spoilt everything for me, persuading Aunt E. not to let me stay. And the reason I wanted to stay,' she finished gratuitously but with determination, 'was because I happen to like the place. Not because you were around. You were part of the set-up I could easily have done without, as just two minutes in your company alone were enough to prove.'

There was a short silence. Reya breathed deeply and half wished she had maintained a dignified silence. The past was well and truly the past, after all, and she and Jackson had positively no part in each other's future. But after a moment he said frowningly, 'I guess I deserved that. Yes, I reckon I did.'

She discovered there were tears in her eyes, and she looked blindly through the window, blinking hard. When her vision cleared, she saw a red kangaroo bounding along by the fence at the side of the road, and calmed herself by taking a conscious pleasure in watching the graceful movements of the creature. Her first kangaroo since she had come back! For a second she thought of Warren. He would enjoy that sight too. All the same, she didn't really want him to come to Coolabah Creek . . .

'Enjoying the sight of the green grass?' Jackson asked her presently, and she felt relieved at the normality of his tone.

'Yes. I've never seen it so beautiful.'

43

'A few weeks and it will be gone, so don't get too goggle-eyed over the fabulous outback, you still haven't a clue as to its real nature.' Listening, she sighed. He was still intent on picking at her. 'Did you know we've just had almost three years of drought conditions here?' he continued conversationally. 'Did your aunt tell you we've had to cut down our labour force—that she hasn't had a holiday at the coast the last three summers? Or that we've all grown ten years older while you've been ageing at the usual rate? That's what this country does to us. I told you it was brutal, didn't I?'

Reya looked at him warily, not liking to think of Aunt E. having such a hard time, yet sure he was merely trying to frighten her off. She said with a shrug, 'You don't look to have aged ten years.'

His mouth lifted in a slight smile. 'I believe you're trying to flatter me. Well, I was speaking loosely——'

'About the drought too?' she asked, gaining confidence. 'All that grass——'

'Yes, all that grass. So the drought's over,' he agreed. 'We've had rain—lots of it. But you'd have known all about it if you'd been here a few months ago—it was as dry and waterless as hell. Come to think of it, it's a pity you didn't pay your visit then. It might have been the best thing that could have happened to you. Drought and hard work and heartbreak. There'd have been no to-do then about going back to the green fields of England. Those stars in your eyes wouldn't ever again have lit up at the magic of the word Outback. It would be somewhere you'd want to forget—but fast.'

So it was well and truly on again, she thought. There was to be another campaign to keep Reya Barberton out of *his* country. She wished Aunt E. had told her about the drought. Yet why should she have? At that time, Reya was firmly ensconced in England. But this man, Jackson Brand, he was so determined to put her off. Maybe the country would look desolate and frightening under drought conditions—maybe life would be hard then. But it would be another face of

44

land, and if you have a passion for the land, even if it's a secret passion, and you're half suspicious of it yourself, then you want to see every aspect of it. It could be like—loving a man, reflected Reya, shivering slightly. There would be sides to his personality that baffled you, that frightened you, but because they were part of him, then you had to know them and to accept them. But what hope would she ever have of explaining to someone as prejudiced against her as Jackson Brand was how she felt about a country that he saw as his, but most definitely not as hers?

She said slowly, 'I can face facts. I also know a little about hard work. I haven't spent all my life being waited on——'

He made no reply to that, and she stole a glance at him and was aware of a confusion in her emotions. That tough dark sinewy look—was that what drought had done to him? Hard times—overwork—worry. It wasn't just the passing of four years, it wasn't just that she had partly forgotten how he looked. She felt an almost intolerable sense of alienation—of being on the outside and not even allowed to look in. It hurt her somewhere in the region of her heart, and shockingly, she knew an urge to touch the thick dark curling hair that lay against his neck—an urge that she had consciously to resist.

He drove on, appearing quite unaware of her, and Reya stared at him for a long moment, his dark profile etched against the paling sky. It was cooler now, there was a soft warm wind, and the colour of the sky, though pallid, had a reflection of red fire in it that was echoed in the stiff tufts of grass in the paddocks. They were driving along wheel tracks now, and they still had a long way to go. It would be dark before they reached Coolabah Creek. It had always been dark when they arrived and the sight of the lights at the homestead when at last they were nearly there had always given her a thrill. She thought with concern of her aunt and uncle and the bad years they had experienced. Despite all Jackson Brand had said, she wished she could have been there then—to help, to share—and she wondered if she would find them aged.

She sighed a little and made herself say, 'I didn't know about the drought or that you've been short-handed. I should—I should apologise about today—for making myself such a nuisance——'

He gave her a surprised look. 'Don't bother. We'll call it quits.' He reached for another cigarette. 'Whatever comes up, we can deal with it—in our own way.'

She said out of her thoughts, 'Girls like Marlene, who've been brought up here—they can cope.'

He couldn't have heard because he didn't comment, and after that they were both quiet. The sun was almost flat to the horizon and visibility was low because of the dust that floated red and dazzling between them and the sun as they made a turn that brought them facing due west. Something leaped across in front of the station wagon, and Reya gasped as Jackson uttered an oath that made her ears tingle. The car swerved and slowed and swerved again as another great dark shadow loomed, then she saw two kangaroos, one behind the other, bounding along by the fence.

The car picked up speed again and the man beside her said, his voice brittle, 'Wouldn't do to collect a 'roo on the windscreen. They're a menace at this time of evening.' After a second he added, 'Sorry about the language. It's apt to slip out in a crisis—not fit for innocent ears like yours, it's a fact. I'll guarantee your friend Warren Livingston-Lee——'

'Lowe,' she corrected.

'Lowe, then—has better manners than I have. Quite your type of man, in fact.'

'I didn't get the impression you liked him particularly when you met him yesterday.'

He shrugged. 'We belong to different worlds, that's all. As you and I do. How long have you decided to stay with us, by the way? With summer coming on—and it's going to be a hot summer—I'd recommend you make it brief.'

'Would you? Well, it will be for Aunt E. to decide how long she wants me to stay.' She reflected as she said it that last time it hadn't been for Aunt E. to say. 'I'll stay for the wedding anyhow,' she added flippantly. 'I wouldn't miss that for a fortune.'

His eyebrows rose. 'Well, I suppose an outback wedding's something of an event,' he conceded. Reya felt she had scored a point there somehow, though it was not a very major one.

Soon they passed the turn-off to Big Sky homestead, and then it was not long before the lights of Coolabah Creek came into view. Reya sat tensely on the edge of her seat. Soon she was going to discover if she had been clinging to something ephemeral that would dissolve into nothingness or if—or if she, Reya Barberton, really was hooked for good and all on the outback. Already the world she had left behind her seemed vague and shadowy, Warren Livingston-Lowe was little more than a name, his extraordinary proposal an illusion. The weeks on board ship had vanished—last night was forgotten. The future she had longed for had become the present.

CHAPTER THREE

To Reya's relief, Jackson didn't stay more than long enough to unload her luggage and exchange a few words with Tom and Elaine Westwood. Then with an indifferent gesture of farewell to Reya, he was gone and she stood on the lighted verandah with her uncle and aunt.

Aunt E. was full of smiles and delighted exclamations. 'You've quite grown up, Reya—and such a pretty girl! I always knew you'd blossom. But you look worn out, darling, after that long drive.'

'I feel wonderful,' Reya protested. There were no reproaches and recriminations about her not having come yesterday, and for that she was grateful. She looked at her aunt searchingly, seeing her with new eyes, and certainly there were lines on her rather plump pretty face that she didn't remember, and the red-gold hair, drawn back into a loose knot, looked as though it would be better for a good styling.

Uncle Tom, however, appeared to her to have changed very little despite Jackson's statement regarding the trials of the drought. He was a broad-shouldered, thick-set man with hair that was prematurely silver—as far as she remembered, it had always been silver, and it contrasted strongly with his tanned face. He was shorter and heavier than Jackson, and to Reya he looked a very fit and healthy man. He had always struck Reya as the type of man whom nothing would worry—an easy-going, comfortable sort of man. She had memories of him coming in around sunset to sit on the verandah with E. and enjoy a glass or two of cold beer. His was a man's world and E. kept everything just the way he liked it in the homestead. He was, Reya supposed, her aunt's whole life, particularly as she had no children. 'I'm a home body,' she used to say. She never went out riding, she had nothing to do with the sheep, but she was quite wrapped up in her home and garden—baking bread, even, 'because Tom so loves it home-baked and it's a skill I've acquired'. There were always fresh flowers in the vases and clean linen on the beds, and the tableware sparkled.

Tonight, after Reya had settled into that room that had always been hers—Lesley and Jean had each had a separate bedroom too—they had a late dinner. Aunt E. commented over the roast lamb, 'Looking after those children must have been hard work. Though Jackson said he rather thought you'd had some help with them,' she added with a little knowing smile.

Reya smiled back but didn't go into it. It sounded as if Jackson had formed his own opinion of her relationship with Warren and passed it on to E. Just now she didn't feel like talking about Warren Livingston-Lowe. Possibly she would tell E. about him one of these days, but not tonight. Tonight she was—home, and she sighed a little and said, without really caring about it any more, 'Jackson said I was a nuisance, coming today instead of yesterday. I'm truly sorry about that.'

'You should have stayed in Sydney longer,' E. said. 'But it's lovely to see you.'

'Sorry we didn't meet you,' Tom remarked. 'But Jackson insisted on taking the blame—said he should have strong-armed you one way or the other yesterday.'

One way or the other? To come at once—or not to come at all? Was Jackson supposed to have that much power? Reya wondered.

'I wouldn't be strong-armed,' she admitted. 'I'd promised —these people I'd spend some time with them,' she concluded somewhat falsely, and observing E.'s amused look, she flushed and wondered what on earth Jackson had said.

E. took her up on the point next morning after Tom had departed and the homestead was quiet. The house girl was washing the dishes and E., who had insisted that Reya should have breakfast in bed, was sitting on the chintz-covered chair by the long glass doors that opened on to the verandah.

'These *people* you promised to spend time with, Reya—were they parents, relatives of the man you met on the ship?'

Reya had left her bed and was gathering her toilet things ready to take a shower. She said resignedly, 'No, they were English friends of Warren's.'

'Oh. Tell me about Warren, do. He sounded darling from what Jackson said.'

'There's nothing to tell,' Reya said after a moment. She pushed back her sheeny dark hair, then drew a comb through it. 'You know how people get sort of friendly on a voyage—you're thrown together and you need the company, and you think you're lucky if you find someone really congenial.'

'You sound such a seasoned traveller,' E. said, smiling fondly. 'And I think you were very lucky—really lucky. Jackson said you'd want to go back to Sydney—that you wouldn't want to stay long with us.'

'Did he?' Reya couldn't keep a touch of asperity from her voice. 'Well, I don't know where he got that idea, because what I've been looking forward to most of all is coming here.' She moved over to the glass doors and looked out across the garden where the blossoming orange trees were buzzing with bees, and the paddocks behind were a billowing green. 'How long will it be like that?'

'The grass?' Her aunt spoke absently, a little sadly. 'A few weeks. Then the sun will dry it all up and it'll be the red and brown land we're used to.' She continued after a moment, 'Reya, I know this is an unpopular subject and that you've come a long way to see us, but you mustn't become too fond of the outback. I do appreciate the company and affection of my niece, but you're *young*—you must be where you'll meet people, young people, young men who belong in your sort of world—like this Warren.' She stopped and spread her hands, practical hands with rounded nails. '*That's* why Jackson thinks you shouldn't be encouraged to come here except for a sensibly short term."

Reya listened incredulously. Jackson interfering again! By what right?

'In fact,' E. said a little uncomfortably, 'when he went down to Sydney he intended to tell you not to come out west at all.'

'Did *you* ask him to tell me that, Aunt E?'

'Well, no, darling. But I talked to him about it. I had the feeling you might want to stay a long time, and after all, it is important for a girl to move in the right milieu.'

'You have been brainwashed,' Reya thought. 'By Jackson Brand.' Because hadn't Aunt E., once an English girl with a background not much different from Reya's, settled down happily in the outback? So shouldn't she sympathise with Reya? But Jackson Brand had to horn in once again and practically say that the outback was out of bounds for Reya. It was hurtful and it was unfair, but this time it was just too bad for Jackson Brand, he was going to discover that he couldn't always manipulate people. Meanwhile, she could hardly wait for the wedding, so that he would go away on his honeymoon and stop persecuting her. And she fervently hoped that this time Marlene wouldn't change her mind and run off with someone else—though she wouldn't blame her very much if she did!

'This man you met on the ship,' E. was saying. 'It might sound calculating, darling, but I really wouldn't advise you to stay away from Sydney long. Certainly not on my account, much as I love you and enjoy your company.'

'Aunt,' Reya said firmly, 'you're imagining it if you think you can hear wedding bells for me.' She debated for a moment whether she would say anything about Warren's proposal, then decided against it because it was just a little unbelievable, and she was practically certain she wasn't going to follow it up. 'I hardly know Warren. We only met on the ship, and that's a very artificial environment.'

'That's true, darling, and it really carries out what I'm saying. You should give yourself a chance to get to know him in normal everyday surroundings. Jackson says he's your kind of person.'

Jackson says! Reya wanted to scream. She asked exasperatedly, 'For heaven's sake—how would Jackson know? They only said How-do-you-do to each other on the wharf!'

E.'s palely pencilled eyebrows rose and she was suddenly a little on her dignity. 'Jackson is an excellent judge of human nature, Reya,' she said severely. 'I'd trust his judgment above that of any man I know—except for Tom's,' she added, but it was plainly out of loyalty to Tom.

Reya sighed. 'Have it your own way, Aunt E. But I do wonder what my relationships with other people have to do with Jackson Brand. Or any other part of my life either, come to that . . . And now I'd better have my shower, and if there's nothing particular I can do for you, I'd like to go out for a ride.'

'Do that, darling,' agreed E. forgivingly. 'Blackberry Tart is yours to ride whenever you wish. You must enjoy yourself while you're here, and I suppose—if nothing does come of your friendship with Warren—that you have plans for going back home eventually?'

Home. To England. When Reya's heart was insistent still that home was here in the outback of Australia. She said lightly, 'I'm playing it by ear, Aunt.'

She reflected a little sadly as she took her shower that she and her aunt didn't really know each other very well. She was beginning to suspect Aunt E. of a certain weakness of character, and as for herself—she had been a schoolgirl and a fairly secretive one at that, those other years, so how could her aunt know the depth of her hopes and desires?

When she came through the house half an hour later wearing white jeans and a pink cotton shirt, Marlene Newell had just driven up to the homestead. To discuss the feeding of the guests at her wedding breakfast, thought Reya, aware of an odd feeling in the pit of her stomach. Unworthily, she decided she would leave it all to Aunt E. She would help with the preparation when the time came, but she just didn't want to be involved in plans and discussions. Yes, on reflection the topic of Marlene's and Jackson's wedding had no appeal for her at all. She would sooner go for a ride.

All the same, before she knew what had happened, Aunt E. appeared with a tray of freshly baked scones and a huge pot of tea, and the three of them were making their way to a small table on the verandah.

'It didn't take *you* long to get here,' commented Marlene, looking Reya over with eyes that were not even as friendly and welcoming as Jackson's had been. Or was it only Reya's imagination that made her think that? She had only ever encountered Marlene a couple of times before and didn't remember her terribly well—more from the wedding photograph she had seen in the press than from actual meetings, in fact. She was taller than Reya, lightly tanned with lustrous brown hair, a square forehead and a determined chin. Her eyes were light blue and widely set under well-marked eyebrows and knowledgeable rather than innocent. Her figure was trim and as she moved towards a chair, Reya observed that she had a decided, though indolent, swagger.

It was curious how the two girls examined each other quickly and thoroughly—as though they were rivals in some way, which of course they were not. Reya squirmed inwardly, feeling overdressed in her white pants and pretty blouse, while Marlene was ultra-casual in faded blue jeans and checked shirt, her sunglasses pushed up into her hair. No need for effort from Marlene because this was the world into which she had been born and to which she quite obviously still belonged, even if she had deserted it for the nickel fields of Western Australia for a few years.

E. poured the tea and Marlene reached for her cup and took a scone. 'I had the idea you weren't to honour us with your company at all,' she remarked, following up her earlier comment.

Reya gritted her teeth. *Us.* That meant herself and Jackson. And her company—at the wedding. She smiled determinedly, aware that her teeth at any rate were a whole lot prettier than Marlene's, whose teeth were rather uneven. 'Oh, there was never any doubt about my coming. And it will be a—a thrill to help with the wedding,' she concluded brightly.

Marlene stared at her thoughtfully, then raised her cup and sipped her tea, and transferred her attention to E. Almost without being aware of it, Reya observed she still wore a wide gold wedding ring and nothing else on her left hand.

'I want to talk about that, E.,' she said in her unaffected slightly flat voice, and Reya nervily recalled her own earlier decision to opt out of menu planning. 'There's just no sense at all in your doing the catering, you know.'

'My dear,' E. interrupted firmly—so firmly that Reya wondered at herself for ever thinking E. was a weak character, 'Jerry asked me to do it. He and Trisha agreed that it would be the most convenient arrangement.'

'Oh, Trisha!' said Marlene contemptuously. 'That woman's made a complete monkey out of my father. He acted like a silly old man falling for someone young enough to be his daughter. It makes me furious the way he panders to her every whim—the daughter of a small town tradesman, the sort of person one simply doesn't meet—and here she is queening it in Susan's and my home ... *Of course* he asked you to do the catering—he knows damned well she's incapable of it, that all she can do is look pretty—I'll give her *that*. No children, no responsibilities—talk about sit on a cushion and sew a fine seam!' She bit into a scone angrily and presently resumed, 'If she was worth her salt she'd have been working beside Father on the property during the drought. *I'd* have helped him—*I'd* have done my bit——'

Reya, her tea forgotten, listened feeling slightly stunned. She had known Marlene didn't have a high opinion of her stepmother, but she hadn't known she was as contemptuous of her as this. And she rather thought it was in bad taste to speak so disparagingly of her in front of a comparative stranger, like herself. Even E. was looking severe.

'That's not a fair criticism, Marlene. You should be thankful your father is happy—and make no mistake, he *is* happy.

As for helping with the stock—I didn't help Tom, I'm not capable, and I don't feel guilty about it. I did my bit in other ways, just as Trisha did. We don't all have your capabilities, your stamina, you know. We're all individuals with our own weaknesses—yes, and with our own virtues and special values too. Ask your father about that.'

Marlene raised her eyebrows. 'Oh, you don't have to make excuses for yourself. You're not an Australian, but no one will deny you have virtues, and let's face it, you and Tom come into a slightly different category from us. But for *my father* to have lowered his standards—it's sickening, particularly when you consider that my mother—his first wife —was a bushwoman from pioneer stock. At Lilli-Pilli—at Big Sky—we have traditions. Jackson and I are fourth generation Australians. But this little upstart——' She stopped short and looked suddenly at Reya. 'What brought *you* back here anyway?' she asked, as if, Reya thought wryly, the turn the conversation had taken had brought her to mind, another person who didn't belong and of whom little could be expected—exactly Jackson's opinion. She felt edgy about that remark of Marlene's, subtly patronising, that Tom and E. came into a different category.

She hadn't found an answer to Marlene's rudely abrupt question when the other girl continued, 'The wedding can hardly be that big a draw, and I thought from what Jackson said that you were cosily entrenched in Sydney with your boy-friend, and likely to remain so.'

Reya was exasperated. Warren certainly appeared to have been assigned a very definite role by Jackson Brand. She said coolly, 'Did you? Then you must have misunderstood. Jackson knows that Coolabah Creek was always my ultimate objective.'

Marlene scowled and pushed her tea cup away. She lit a cigarette and blew smoke out of one side of a mouth that seemed to Reya hard and far from young. Marlene, she reflected, must be about thirty. She had been married and widowed. She had the face, the eyes, of experience. Did Jackson not mind that someone else had taught the arts of love to the woman he was going to marry? Her thoughts shocked her, taking her unawares, and she remembered vividly and unexpectedly the warmth and weight of his body on hers that day long ago—when she had been so young . . .

'Ultimate?' said Marlene with a faint and cynical smile. 'Are you getting ideas about belonging here? There aren't really any eligible males around,' she warned. 'Not even in my father's age group.'

Reya swallowed down a mixture of anger and shock. That was a calculated insult, after what she had said about Trisha. She glanced at E., who had either not been aware of it or was acting as if she hadn't. Marlene, her eyes wide open and fixed stonily on Reya's face, blew smoke slowly, so that Reya turned away and coughed and tried not to think of Jackson, who could have been designated an eligible male. But of course no longer.

Marlene, offhand and very cool, said, 'Take my advice and stick to your own scene . . . Do you have a career of some sort? I don't think I ever heard what you took up, did I?'

'I wouldn't know what you heard,' said Reya, and nearly added, 'Except that you heard a few pretty inaccurate things about me.' 'Actually, I took a diploma in Housecraft when I was in England.'

Marlene stared. She seemed on the point of laughing. 'Not really! Good heavens, if you'd been brought up in the outback as I was, you'd have been practically born with the knowledge of how to run a household. It's the pioneer in us—it gives us a sort of inborn ability to do anything and everything as it comes up. Of course, people like my step-mother come under a different heading.' Like you, she might as well have added, but she proceeded to ignore Reya and turned back to E. to say briskly, 'To return to our *moutons*—I want to ask you not to start *anything* to do with the wedding yet with or without the help of your accredited niece. As Trisha won't—and can't—manage it I'm quite determined on handling the catering myself. I'm perfectly capable. After all, I've been using that kitchen range since I was a child, and Lilli-Pilli's still my home.'

'No, Marlene,' E. interrupted with sudden and unexpected firmness. 'There I must contradict you. Lilli-Pilli ceased to be your home in any true sense of the word the day you married Teddy Newell and went away to Western Australia. Whether you like it or not, it's Trisha's home now—Trisha's and your father's—and it's for them to make the wedding arrangements, not you. You are simply not to interfere. You'll only make trouble for everyone, and it's not fair to Jerry.'

If Reya hadn't been all too aware of being an outsider, she might at this point have suggested that in all fairness surely Marlene had a right to some say in her own wedding arrangements. But she held her tongue, and the protest came from Marlene, who said heatedly, 'Interfere? You think I should sit back and take it while that woman makes a complete mess of my only sister's wedding?'

Reya stared, unable to comprehend for a moment what she had heard. 'My sister's wedding.' *Susan's* wedding? For a second she thought it was Susan Ramsey who was marrying Jackson, and then, quite crazily, she realised that Jackson didn't come into it at all. Her feelings were suddenly chaotic, she couldn't sort them out. She had taken it all for granted, been so sure it was Marlene and Jackson who were to be married. She had, in fact, jumped to conclusions.

Absently, she noticed Marlene's hand tremble as she put a cigarette to her lips and drew on it. Marlene was fighting against her stepmother's arrangements for her sister's wedding, Marlene wasn't the bride after all, and suddenly it all seemed perfectly logical. Because, despite all her other feelings about Jackson, despite the fact that he had fallen very smartly from the pedestal on which she had romantically set him as a sixteen-year-old, Reya did have a certain respect for him. He was a man of stature, a man to be reckoned with, and it would be strangely out of character if he were to pick up the threads again so nonchalantly with a girl who had once jilted him. If Marlene wanted him back, then she would have to work hard to win him. Well, she was welcome to try—and she would be welcome to him if she somehow made it.

The thing was, as far as Reya Barberton was concerned, that now there was no honeymoon in sight for Jackson Brand, she would have to suffer his presence around the place after all, and that was just too bad. In fact, it was a bore, and she moved restlessly in her chair and stared out to the far horizon where a single long, low, flat-topped range lay like a blue shadow against the pale blue of the sky. She thought vaguely, 'I'd like to ride out there,' and had a vivid mental image of herself on Blackberry Tart's back flying out across the paddock through the long grasses and over the tussocks of bluebush and umbrella bush . . .

Aunt E., who had been saying something about oiled wheels, now proceeded temperately, 'There'll be no confusion at all, Marlene. Susie will have a lovely wedding, and no one will even know that the wedding breakfast wasn't cooked in the Lilli-Pilli kitchen, and if they did it's no slur on anyone—on Trisha or Jerry or on you either. Why, in the city, lots of women have the catering done professionally. It's only sense when there's a big reception.'

'The city!' Marlene's eyes blazed with scorn. 'We're outback people and we always have been. We like things done in outback style—with lavish hospitality, the doors thrown open and a big welcome for everyone. I gave up my dreams of a proper country style wedding because of Trisha. I knew she was just too lazy and selfish to bother. She just isn't one of us, she's a small town type who doesn't have a clue what our life style is. Well, it's not going to happen to Susie!'

'Now, Marlene,' said E. good-humouredly, 'you're being melodramatic. You can hardly blame Trisha for *your* wedding arrangements, you know very well it was such a whirlwind affair you barely even let anyone know it was going to happen before it was all an accomplished fact. Susie will have her bush wedding with all the trimmings, even though she's become a city girl and is going to spend the rest of her life in the city,' she added ironically. 'Trisha will have the homestead shining and beautiful—there'll be flowers from that lovely garden——'

'Flowers my father and I grew,' snapped Marlene. 'And the housegirls will do all the cleaning and polishing regardless of my pretty stepmother. No one will be invited to stay overnight—they'll all have to camp in their cars or go off to Djilla.'

'I don't know anything about that,' said E. firmly. 'But I don't like the way you're talking about Trisha. What must Reya think? She's a very sweet person and she's your father's wife, and you should be more discreet, particularly in the company of——'

She stopped, and Reya wondered what she had been going to say. The company of a stranger, an outsider?

But E. was smiling, her head with its long slightly untidy swathe of red-gold hair a little on one side. 'Oh dear, I was going to say children,' she said ruefully. 'I can't get used to your being grown up, Reya—nearly twenty-one years old.'

Marlene's eyes were bright and her cheeks flushed. 'You never liked me, did you, E.? You're loyal to Trisha. Your trouble is that you're neither fish nor flesh, you don't really belong to the outback fraternity, though you've managed to develop a bit of protective colouring which deceives most people. All the same,' she finished with a hard look, 'I don't think you'd be sorry if Tom asked you to leave Coolabah Creek tomorrow.' Once again, she turned her attention aggressively to Reya. 'Who are you expecting, all dressed up in that smart outfit, anyhow?'

'Nobody,' said Reya. She'd never had an inkling that Marlene would dislike her so much, or that she had the world's population divided quite distinctly into two—those who belonged to the outback, and those who didn't. In that, she reflected wryly, she certainly had something in common with Jackson Brand. He had put Reya on the other side of the fence—with the goats, not the sheep!—and quite obviously in Marlene's view too that was where she belonged —with Trisha. As for E., by some special dispensation it appeared she was kindly allowed to sit on the fence.

'Why don't you get yourself some sensible clothes and learn to ride?' Marlene wanted to know. 'Or are you one of those determinedly feminine types who work on the old principle that the way to a man's heart is through his stomach?'

Reya itched to slap her face. She said quietly, 'I can ride already, Marlene, and as far as I'm aware there's not a man around here whose heart is worth aiming for—whether it's via his stomach or any other part of his anatomy.'

E. gasped very slightly, and Marlene blinked her widely spaced pale blue eyes and stood up.

'Keep thinking that way,' she said crisply. 'It'll be better for your health.' She smiled, but it wasn't a friendly smile. 'By which I mean you're a city girl, aren't you? . . . Meanwhile, I'm going to hunt up Jackson and see what *his* opinion is about this wedding breakfast business. I'm perfectly willing to abide by *his* decision.'

E. looked at her wryly. 'My opinion doesn't have much weight with you, does it? See Jackson, then.'

Marlene merely shrugged and tossed a casual goodbye over her shoulder as she left the house and went back to her car.

E. watched her drive away. 'Poor Marlene! She's not a very tactful girl. It was a tragedy she lost her husband, but I do hope she doesn't make trouble at Lilli-Pilli. She couldn't live at peace with Trisha before, and she can't do so now. She shouldn't have come back, but of course there's Susie's wedding. The ideal solution would be for her to marry again.'

Jackson? Reya wondered. She suspected it was he who had brought her back rather than her sister's wedding, and she wondered what her chances were—and what Marlene considered the surest way to a man's heart.

E. took the tray out to the kitchen and Reya went down to the horse-paddock to ask Spence to saddle up Blackberry Tart. On consideration, she supposed her white pants weren't really very suitable for riding and she couldn't quite work out why she had put them on. However, she wasn't going to change just because of something Marlene had said.

Spence was the general hand at Coolabah Creek, and he had been here for years. He was short and sharp-eyed and quick, despite the fact he had a pronounced limp, the result of an accident while riding. He was one of those men who are completely devoted to the outback. Reya simply couldn't imagine him living anywhere else, just as she couldn't imagine Tom or Jackson or Marlene in a more civilised setting, permanently, that was.

'G'day, Reya,' Spence greeted her, removing the cigarette that hung perpetually on his lower lip. 'How you going? I bet I know what horse you're after——'

Reya grinned. 'I'm fine, thanks, Spence. I bet you do know too. How is she? Growing old?'

'I reckon no more than the rest of us.' Spence laconically replaced his cigarette and strolled across the yard. 'No, Reya, Blackberry's still a bonzer little mare—bred over at Big Sky, so what would you expect? Just hang on a mo while I saddle her up and you'll be in business. Where you going?'

'Just for a ride,' said Reya. It was news to her that the boss of Big Sky had bred Blackberry Tart. She hadn't known Uncle Tom bought his horses from there, but she wasn't going to let it spoil her pleasure in the little mare. She determinedly wiped her mind clear of people and personalities and problems—she had always been able to do that at Coolabah Creek, it was one of the charms of the place, part of the spell it put upon her. She leaned against the rail and waited for Spence. She could smell wattle blossom on the sunny air as well as that intangible scent of eucalyptus leaves. She hadn't realised till now just how integral a part of the landscape these scents were for her, and as in a dream she took her fill of them and through half closed eyes looked down towards the creek where the coolabahs and river red gums and wattle trees grew. A half turn of her head brought the homestead bungalow into view, unpretentious with its red painted, galvanised iron roof and slender straight verandah posts. Aunt E.'s garden was neat and orderly with citrus trees at one side and pepper trees at the other, plus a small vegetable garden that she tended herself.

But curiously, with her mind's eye, Reya was looking at another station homestead—the one at Big Sky. A long low silver-roofed building, its colour old ivory, its verandah roof curving elegantly down to make extra shade. Reya had never been inside that bungalow, but she had sat on the verandah where the oleanders crowded in, their red and rose and white flowers elusively honey-scented. And it was on that verandah that Jackson Brand had crushed her body beneath his . . .

Reya turned from her thoughts, suddenly sickened. Why couldn't she forget all that? It had been a traumatic experience at the time—all of it. The destruction of an idol and a dream, the first encounter with a man's passion. But at nearly twenty-one, she surely knew enough to relegate it to a very minor position in her life's experiences. Nothing drastic had happened, after all—she wasn't going to persuade herself it had given her some kind of a hang-up.

She uttered a brief exclamation of disgust at herself and glanced at her watch. The time told her nothing, yet in her mind was the awareness that at this moment, Marlene Newell was quite probably discussing her sister's wedding reception with Jackson. Without doubt she would get some advice from him. Jackson Brand was great on handing *that* out, and Reya hoped it would be advice that Marlene found palatable. As far as she was concerned, he had never yet managed to produce any advice that was even vaguely acceptable . . .

Presently Spence helped her into the saddle and she was off across the paddock. The sun shone down hotly on her back and on her head and she felt the old spell encompassing her—riding under this wide sky with the horizon stretching out for ever, ahead of her the pale landscape—pale green now, with bluish trees and the waters of a tank reflecting back the pallor of the sky, and merinos gathering in the shade of a tall box tree. She remembered as she rode the deep thrill of coming upon Jackson Brand riding one of

62

his beautiful horses, his wide-brimmed hat pushed back from his brow, a couple of dogs at his horse's heels. And she remembered the moment when she and Jean and Lesley were close enough to see the blue of those eyes that flicked them a casual ironical glance. Jean had always talked animatedly, but Reya had held her breath and feasted her eyes. No wonder that face was etched so deeply in her mind!

Yet in what contempt he must have held her—a silly romantic little schoolgirl. He had believed *she* was the one who had tracked him down—and he had killed her delicate awakening emotions by his brutal treatment of her.

And incidentally, killed stone dead her belief in him as some sort of a hero.

'*Stone* dead,' she said aloud, angry that Jackson Brand impinged so continually on her remembered and lovely dreamtime. Some chockalotts flew out of the coolabah trees with a screech and she dug her heels into Blackberry Tart's sides so that the little mare broke into a gallop.

CHAPTER FOUR

SHE saw absolutely nothing of Jackson Brand for several days. Rather strangely, just as being in love with him had given life at Coolabah Creek a special tingling excitement and intensity in the old days, so now she discovered that her very antagonism towards him, even the thought that her presence was obnoxious to him, seemed to stimulate her. She hadn't quite got used to the fact that he wasn't to be married to Marlene, and she wanted to see him rather than avoid him. When it didn't happen, she felt deprived, cheated.

What had been the outcome of his and Marlene's discussion of the wedding breakfast arrangements, she had no idea. E. didn't mention it, but simply went ahead with her plans as though nothing had happened, flicking through dog-eared cookery books, her glasses on the end of her nose; now and then at the oddest moments making trips to her larder to survey the shelves, shift jars and canisters and packets and exclaim in either triumph or exasperation.

The menu, when it emerged, was delectable, with hot entrées, various meats and salads and side dishes, and sweets that included the Australian favourite, Pavlova, a concoction of meringue and cream and fruit salad that Reya had often enjoyed when she had stayed with E. before. Reya thought they must be going to feed a multitude, and E. said with satisfaction, 'Yes, the table will be groaning—that's bush hospitality.'

Soon they would have to make a shopping expedition to Djilla, but meanwhile Reya went out riding daily, to rediscover her dreamtime in the sweep of the tantalisingly ugly-beautiful plains that had long ago cast their spell upon her. Always she found herself hoping that she would encounter Jackson Brand and have the pleasure of annoying him with her nonchalant presence. But she didn't see him, and it was maddening.

One afternoon she had been watching her uncle and Mack and their kelpie dogs mustering some sheep into another paddock, but at last she rode off restlessly on her own, looking, she supposed, for trouble. In other words, for Jackson Brand. Deliberately she rode in the direction of Big Sky, taking a track that she and the other girls had followed often that last year. She had always enjoyed riding Blackberry Tart and now, riding in the hot sunshine across an enormous paddock that looked like open parkland with its green cover and its clumps of belah and cyprus and wilga trees, she felt her nerves tingle with a pleasure that was half nostalgic pain. In her heart, the mare was hers, the parkland was hers, and she thought she could live here for ever. In the distance, the waters of a brimming tank reflected the blue of the sky, and Reya rode on until she could see the line of the creek as it curved round again, its course marked by coolabahs and river red gums. Her nostrils caught the musty, dusty, haunting scent of the wattle, and she could see the glow of the creamy blossoms with an occasional Gold Dust adding its fervent burning yellow, while on the ground, Sturt's Desert Pea flung out a sprawling patch of spectacular red and black flowers.

Reya reached the shade of the trees and dismounted to walk by the creek. Cicadas drummed, magpies warbled, and she looked fascinated at the brown water surging along the creek-bed that in other years had held nothing but a string of potholes. She loved this land. If it claimed you, it claimed you body and soul, and that was a fact. She wanted to be able to say, 'This is my land—this land that tolerates man's presence here and grudgingly accords him a living.' She wondered suddenly, for no particular reason, if Jackson thought she had come back here with an eye to the main chance—that she was hoping, because her aunt and uncle had no children, that they would leave Coolabah Creek to her. Her own thought shocked her, for such a thing had never entered her head for a single moment before, and now she wished the thought hadn't come to her.

A little troubled, she stood with lowered head brooding over her thoughts, and then something made her look up. Startlingly, Jackson Brand appeared through the trees—astride a horse as black as Blackberry Tart, but taller, bigger, a stallion. He had seen her, and in a moment he had swung down from the saddle and was striding towards her. He was bareheaded and his curling black hair gleamed in the sunlight with an indescribable richness. It was as sheeny as the flanks of his horse. His skin looked dark as teak and his blue eyes were unavoidable, and Reya was aware of a feeling that was almost panic. She had wanted this encounter, but now her legs were suddenly weak, her whole body had gone slack and there was clamour in her mind.

She stood staring silently while he stared back at her as he came nearer, and eventually stopped within a few feet of her.

He felt for cigarettes, but his eyes didn't leave her, skimming over her short-sleeved red shirt and black jeans to come back to her face. Then he said in a casual conversational tone, 'In that red and black gear with your head bowed, you remind me of the faithful little native girl waiting for her lover.'

Reya blinked. She had expected attack of some sort and now she was at a loss for words. He gave his attention to lighting his cigarette and then his blue eyes again met hers directly.

'Do you know the legend?'

'No.' Her heart had begun to leap about in her bosom quite alarmingly, and as she stared at his lean muscular torso, she remembered again the one and only time her body had been in close contact with his. Why she had to think of it now she didn't know, and instantly she had the ridiculous feeling that he could read her thoughts. He could do a number of offbeat things, she knew—things like water-divining and tracking. He could track almost as well as a native. The first time she had ever visited the outback he had found a child who had been lost. That perhaps had been a significant beginning to her knowledge of him—the hero who found the lost girl, and upon whom the weeping mother—it had been the wife of one of the stockmen—had flung herself, kissing his hand in gratitude.

Now he stooped and picked one of the red and black flowers that grew at Reya's feet. He twirled it for an instant, then handed it to her and automatically she took it, though she was annoyed to see her fingers trembling.

'The aboriginals tell a story about this flower. Do you know it?'

'The flower? It's Sturt's Desert Pea.'

'Yes, well, everyone knows that,' he agreed. 'I meant the story. Look here—see these long drooping crimson petals, the round shining black centre? If you use your imagination a little you can see it's a black girl in a red cloak.'

'Yes,' said Reya, interested despite herself.

He continued as if to a child, 'The cloak was made of parrot feathers by the girl's warrior lover who went away with the rest of the tribe. She stayed behind and waited for him faithfully, for long years, but he never returned. Eventually, the dreamtime heroes took pity on her and she was turned into this flower. So let that,' he concluded with an enigmatic and infuriating smile, 'be a lesson to you, Reya Barberton.'

Reya felt herself flush crimson. What on earth was he talking about? She hoped he hadn't got the idea in his head that she was waiting for *him*. Hadn't he caught on yet that she positively and actively returned his dislike?

She stammered out, 'A lesson to me? I don't know what you mean. I don't have a cloak of parrot feathers and—and I'm certainly not waiting for my—for any lover.'

He smiled narrowly as she stumbled over the words. 'All the same,' he said, 'take care that something similar doesn't happen to you. You do invite it, you know.'

'I don't know,' she retorted. 'You've stretched my imagination well past its limits. I don't even begin to follow you. I'm not aware that I ask for—for disaster of any kind.'

'I think you do. You're a romantic and always have been.'

A romantic! For heaven's sake, was he still working on the idea that she was in love with him? It was certainly time he was disillusioned. She said, 'A romantic? Me? You must think I'm still a silly schoolgirl. I'm a very practical person these days. I've been working in a most realistic way for my living for some time now, even if I am years younger than you. Don't fool yourself you know even the least little thing about me just because I was here a couple of times when I was a teenager.'

He screwed up one blue eye and the other seemed to assess her. Finally he nodded. 'Yes, I can see you've aged,' he said mockingly. 'As for understanding you—you're right, I don't. The thing is, we come from completely different worlds—and never the twain shall meet.'

Message received and understood, she thought wryly. He could certainly twist everything to suit himself! With sudden unwise inspiration she reminded him, 'Still, I do have an aunt who's disproved that old saying with *her* marriage.'

His lips curled up. 'There's such a thing as compromise. And there are always people who'll throw themselves under the wheels of the Juggernaut willingly for one reason or another, love being the usual cause. But sacrifice, unless it remains a secret for ever, can be lethal to true happiness.'

Reya listened and puzzled over what he had said. Surely he didn't think E. had sacrificed herself? She loved Tom and she loved the outback, and Reya was certain she would never want to live anywhere else—even if she was English. E. wasn't suffering in silence . . . She said only, 'I don't care for people who talk in riddles.'

'Well then, let's just say I'm warning you not to lapse back into being romantic and unrealistic now you're here again.'

'I'm in no danger of doing that,' she said, flushing.

'So after the wedding, you'll go.' It was a statement, and not a question.

'Why should I? I like it here . . . What did you and Marlene decide, by the way, about the wedding breakfast?'

'Marlene and I?' His eyebrows shot up. 'Surely you must

68

know what's been arranged. E. is doing the catering as she promised Trisha and Jerry. With you to help her, we can't possibly go wrong, can we?'

Reya shrugged and dropped the flower he had given her, then turned away. 'I'm going back home.'

'You haven't enjoyed my company?'

'You must be joking,' she said.

'I surely must be,' he agreed. 'Still, it was nice running into you.'

'I presume it was accidental,' she said with a touch of malice. 'Though with so many miles to choose from, it's odd our paths should have crossed.'

'I don't know—I often take this way. But I'll admit I saw you in your red shirt from some distance away. Good manners dictated I should stop and say good day.' Their eyes met in a long and inexplicable exchange, then abruptly Reya moved off towards Blackberry Tart. Jackson moved with her and held the stirrup while she mounted.

'You're a graceful little creature,' he said then. 'I remember you riding this mare four years ago when you and your pretty stepsisters used to follow me so relentlessly and we had so many unexpected meetings in such unexpected places. Remember?'

'Yes, I remember,' she said coldly, though her heart was thudding. 'You were Jean's idol—I don't know why. But it's a long while ago, isn't it? These days I'll leave you to manage all the fortuitous meetings—or to avoid them.'

He smiled enigmatically and left her.

As she rode home, Reya knew in her heart that she had been responsible for that particular meeting—just by being on that track. Because she knew it was a track he used frequently, and the discomfiting thing was that *he* knew she knew. It hadn't, at that, been a particularly satisfactory encounter, though it had quietened one part of her mind. She had scored one or two points and so had he, and at least she had made it plain to him that she wouldn't be toddling off meekly after the wedding just because he wanted it.

It now remained to be seen if he would make any move to

see that his so far polite injunctions were carried out . . .

A couple of days later it was arranged that Tom should drive E. to Djilla for the day to buy all the odds and ends on her rather long list. The previous afternoon, Marlene called in at Coolabah Creek, presumably to give her approval or disapproval to E.'s plans. Reya decided to keep diplomatically out of the way. She didn't want to be involved in arguments or differences, though she was quite sure E. was capable of holding her own. She had put away her sparkling white pants since her earlier meeting with Marlene and now made a habit of wearing black or blue, and when she came on to the verandah Marlene was sitting smoking, legs crossed, and listening to whatever E. was saying with an expression on her face that suggested she was about to interrupt—or contradict—at any moment.

She turned to look at Reya when E. paused to ask, 'Are you going for a ride, lovey?'

'I thought I would. Is that all right?'

'Of course. Why don't you go over to the belah paddock? Tom's dipping the wethers and you'll probably see the tail end of the day's work and have company riding home.'

Reya had thought of going down to the creek, and as she hesitated, her aunt added, 'Jackson will be there, I believe.'

For some reason Reya felt a wave of colour sweep into her cheeks. Marlene was looking at her hard and she said, too quickly for thought, 'I don't particularly want to watch the dipping, Aunt E.'

'Please yourself, darling,' E. said agreeably. 'So long as you're happy. Now, Marlene, I've planned this all out very carefully and I think you'll agree——'

Reya moved away down the steps. Why had she said that? Because of course she wanted to go over to the belah paddock—to see the dipping, and, incidentally, to needle Jackson Brand if she could. Bother Marlene! Jackson wasn't her property, and though she had been engaged to him once she wasn't now. Not officially, at any rate.

However, somewhat to her chagrin, she didn't have

the opportunity to needle Jackson after all, because when she reached the belah paddock, where the dip and the shearing sheds were, Jackson Brand simply wasn't around.

Her uncle, Mack, and another man were putting the last of a large mob of wethers through the dip. Tom greeted Reya amiably and she stayed in the saddle half watching and half thinking about Jackson Brand. The holding yard by now was empty and Tom was letting the last of the sheep out of the forcing pen and into the long concrete trough of the dip. Mack and the other man stood one on either side of the race at opposite ends, seeing that the head of each sheep was pushed under as it swam the length of the dip. Reya watched the sheep emerge and stand dripping on the concrete floor of the draining pen, waiting to be let out the gate to join the rest of the mob.

Presently her uncle came out of the yards and walked towards her calling cheerfully, 'I'll leave it to you now, Mack. Tomorrow you'll be on your own to start mustering the wilga paddock. Right?'

They went back to the homestead then, and to Reya's relief, Marlene had gone.

The next day they went to Djilla. It was a small but thriving town serving the sheep stations around the district. You certainly couldn't get everything there, but there was a surprising choice. Tom went off to look up some friends and Reya went shopping with E., who said decidedly, 'For a wedding, only the best will do—and the Ramseys can afford the best. I could have ordered my requirements over the telephone and had the mailman bring them out today, but I prefer to shop around and see for myself. If you want to serve up quality food, then you have to start with top quality ingredients. Isn't that right?'

Reya agreed wholeheartedly that it was, and was henceforth a little amused by her aunt's emphatic and precise hunt for quality.

After they had lunched, E. went eagerly to Jan's Beauty Parlour, where a little to Reya's surprise, she had an appointment to have her hair shampooed and set and her nails manicured. She hadn't before realised that such things had much appeal for her aunt.

While E. was thus occupied, she wandered down the wide main street that was lined with pepper trees. In the one big department store, she sought out the glass and silverware department and looked for some small gift she could buy for Susan and her unknown bridegroom. She was surprised when the girl who came to serve her asked chattily, 'Didn't you used to come in here years ago with Mrs Westwood? You're her niece, aren't you? Here for the wedding, I expect. Are you looking for a gift for the bride?'

'Yes, I am,' admitted Reya with a smile. 'I haven't the least idea what to get. Perhaps you have some suggestions? I don't actually know Susan Ramsey,' she added frankly.

The salesgirl sauntered across to a display table and picking up a small red and gold box, flicked it open. Inside were six coffee spoons with pretty mother-of-pearl handles.

'These are nice,' she offered, and then confided, 'Trisha Ramsey is my cousin, you know.'

Reya was surprised. 'I expect you'll be coming to the wedding, then,' she remarked, examining the spoons approvingly. They seemed to her to be a very suitable choice —a small gift, but in good taste.

The salesgirl laughed and pushed back her red hair. 'Me? Oh lord, no! Jerry wouldn't mind, he's a nice old bloke, but those girls are real snobs. Marlene wouldn't allow Trish to invite any common small town people—she thinks she's just too superior. What's so funny is *she* didn't manage to get herself married off to a wealthy grazier—though she's back for another try, now she's lost her husband. Is she making any progress, do you know?' she asked, maliciously curious.

Reya closed the little gold and red box and handed it back to her. 'I'll take those,' she said, and added coolly, 'I'm afraid I don't know what you're talking about. I haven't been over to Lilli-Pilli.' She smiled as she spoke, but the girl got the message and left the subject alone.

Reya took her small parcel and made her way to the

newsagent's. She could put in a little time there, choosing a few magazines to amuse herself and Aunt E. Then she would buy a box of candies for her aunt, who had a sweet tooth, and after that it should be time to get back to the hairdressers. As she pored over the magazine display, she thought of what the red-headed salesgirl had said—that Marlene hadn't managed to get herself married off to a wealthy grazier—obviously Jackson Brand. Nevertheless, Marlene had been engaged to Jackson—Lesley had picked up that bit of information. And then she had rushed off into a whirlwind romance—E. had used the phrase the other day —with someone else. Reya wondered if she and Jackson had had a lovers' quarrel, or what had happened. She would probably never knew, she thought, as she gathered up the magazines she had selected. It didn't matter one way or the other to her, anyhow. But now she felt quite convinced that Marlene was back for another try, and the very fact that Jackson hadn't married anyone else in the meantime seemed to suggest that her chances could be good—if she handled it in the right way.

'He'd be a tricky man to handle,' she mused as she emerged into the street again. Half aloud, she murmured, 'Good luck to you, Marlene.' Yet she wasn't altogether sure she meant that!

At the hairdresser's she hadn't long to wait before her aunt presented herself with the pleasure and innocence of a child dressed up for a party. A reddish rinse had brightened her hair, which had been set in a style that modified the plump lines of her pretty face, and Reya was more than a little surprised to see how charming and well groomed she could look—no longer the comfortable countrywoman with flyaway hair. As well, of course, she was dressed for town, and wearing high-heeled shoes instead of the flat sandals she wore around the homestead. Reya exclaimed impulsively, 'You look beautiful, Aunt E.!'

Her aunt made a small grimace. 'It won't last. This is just my other self. Not my real self,' she added, sounding just a shade wistful.

Tom, when they ran him to earth in the Courthouse Hotel where he was drinking beer with a group of men, remarked jovially, 'You all know my beautiful wife, don't you? When I see her all dolled up I feel ashamed of myself for not showing her off more often. The life of an outback grazier's wife isn't a very exciting one.'

'Don't be silly, Tom,' E. said, laughing. 'You know I wouldn't change it for anything on earth.'

Reya listened curiously and felt certain E. must feel as she did about the outback—only more so. It wasn't exclusively for third and fourth generation Australians. E. too had spent her girlhood in London, and Reya knew that she and Lynette, who had been Reya's mother, had been brought up in a house in St John's Wood. Their father had been an architect, and he had taken the girls on a world tour after they had completed their education. Reya was vague about the details of the story, but E. had met Tom at a private party and fallen in love with him, and instead of going back to England she had been married. So it was very lucky that she had fallen in love with the outback as well.

Soon after they left Djilla in the car E., sitting in the back seat with Reya, fell asleep, and some time later when they were on the gravel road, the car alarmingly all but crashed into a fence. Tom braked sharply and pulled up, while E., who had been slumped in her corner, sat up with a jerk, eyes wide open.

'What's happened?'

Tom leaned back and drew a hand across his eyes. 'Sorry about that—I dropped off for a second. Too many beers. How about taking over the driving, E.?'

'I wouldn't trust myself, I'm so tired. You have forty winks, Tom, there's no great hurry.'

'My forty winks could last an hour,' said Tom dryly, and Reya offered eagerly, 'Let me drive, Uncle. I have my licence and I'm wide awake. I can't possibly come to any harm—there's not another car in sight.'

'We'd probably end up in Tibooburra,' said Tom good-humouredly. He covered a yawn. 'You've only got to take

74

one wrong track and you'd be lost.'

'If I'm in doubt I'll wake you—or Aunt,' Reya promised. Already she had opened the door and stepped out on to the road. It would really be an experience to try her hand at driving home to Coolabah Creek. The very thought of it was challenging. It was as if the land itself had dared her—and if she refused, then she would have taken her first step back to the cities and that other civilisation. It was a mad thought, yet she knew she *must* take the wheel—prove herself.

Tom had shifted over and as she climbed into the seat beside him he said agreeably, 'All right, we'll give it a go. But mind now—no being too soft-hearted to wake someone if you're in danger of getting bushed.'

She promised again, took a good look at the gear lever and the dashboard, then started up the motor and moved off slowly. She drove extra carefully at first, getting the feel of it all. She had never driven on a gravel road before, actually. She had got her licence while working for the Alfords, and had never done more than take the car down to the shopping centre or to pick up the children from school. She certainly hoped she wouldn't meet up with any kangaroos!

She had gained in confidence and was feeling reasonably at home when Tom dozed off again, and through the rear vision mirror she could see that Aunt E. too had gone off to sleep. She took a deep breath. She was on her own, and she felt curiously exhilarated. She drove on steadily and discovered that she knew exactly where to turn off the gravel and take to the wheel tracks—the stock routes. Only once was she in doubt and then, as she was slowing down, Aunt E. directed from behind her, 'Go to the right here, Reya, or we'll be having dinner at the tank bore in Jackson's eight-mile paddock ... You're doing wonderfully, darling. It's lovely to be sitting back in luxury chauffeured by someone who hasn't had even a single glass of beer.'

It was almost dark when with a sense of triumph and elation Reya pulled up outside the Coolabah Creek garages.

She felt she had learned a little about the country, that she hadn't let it fool her or lead her astray. And next time—next time she would know not to take the track that led to Jackson's eight-mile bore.

It wasn't until she had climbed out of the car that she realised that the vehicle parked under one of the big pepper trees was Jackson Brand's station wagon. Her heart gave a sickening lurch.

Jackson was standing in the half dark on the homestead verandah as they left the car. Tom had come back to life and rather stiffly climbed out and helped carry in the various parcels and packets. Reya saw Jackson looking at her hard —because she had got out of the driver's seat. She sent him back a challenging glance, and told him lightly, 'I've been learning to negotiate outback roads.'

She didn't wait for his reaction, but went straight through to the pantry to deposit her share of the day's purchases. E. followed her, but Tom dumped his portion on the dining room table and proceeded to pour Jackson—and himself—a whisky. Reya knew, because he called out for ice. When she fetched it, he told her cheerily, 'There's some mail here for you, Reya. I hope it's something pleasant. You did a great job just now, I'm proud of you.'

She smiled back, ignoring Jackson, whose attitude seemed dark and forbidding. Her letter was from Warren and she went to the sitting room to read it while the others sat on the verandah with their drinks.

She read the letter quickly, almost impatiently, somehow too conscious of the group on the verandah to give it her full attention. He told her that he was coming to Coolabah Creek. He was on the point of buying a car, and he was going to drive out west and get acquainted with the real Australia. 'I'm not going to pressure you, Reya, but after interviewing a few dollies here I'm more than ever convinced no one will do but you. I shall bring Jon's script with me, and somewhere far from the madding crowd, I shall try to persuade you to try out a few lines of dialogue. I hope I shan't find myself up against opposition from a nest of possessive relatives, and it will be your own decision what you do. If this film turns out well, you and I could have a great association.'

The letter was disturbing. It was like being tempted, because what girl wouldn't feel at least a little tempted by Warren's offer? The thing was, however, apart from the fact that the very thought of acting frightened her, she had this obsessive thing about the outback. If she refused Warren it would quite certainly not be because of the influence of her relatives. She sighed as she folded the pages of the letter and put it back in the envelope. Warren was going to let her know later exactly when he expected to arrive—he supposed that the wedding would be over by then, which was in a way a pity, as it would be quite a thing to attend a wedding at a sheep station.

She was startled when Jackson said from the doorway, 'You're looking pleased. What's the good news?'

'Oh—Warren's coming,' she said, flushing. 'I must ask my aunt if he may stay here.'

'There shouldn't be any doubt about that,' he said dryly, and she walked past him to tell Aunt E. the news.

E. was almost embarrassingly enthusiastic. 'Of course he may come here, darling. I couldn't be more delighted—I'm longing to meet him.'

Reya picked up the gin and tonic that had been poured for her and frowned. She hoped E. wasn't going to be too enthusiastic and wondered if she should tell her that Warren's interest in her, far from being a romantic one, was a business interest. Somehow she didn't think E. would believe that, and as well, she flinched from the thought of mentioning it. The Alfords had already ridiculed her slightly, and though E. was too sweet to do anything so unkind, still she would no doubt be sceptical of the idea—just as Reya herself was sceptical. So she decided the less she said the better, and reminded herself that Warren's name was not likely to mean any more to E. and Tom than it had to Jackson—which was exactly nothing.

'When are we to expect him?' E. asked.

'I'm not sure. He's driving from Sydney, and I suppose he'll take his time. He—he says he'll be in touch.'

'Well, any time will do,' said E. hospitably. 'We'll get a room ready tomorrow, darling.'

Jackson, who didn't seem particularly interested, even though it was he who had put out the idea that Warren was Reya's admirer, changed the subject.

'You ought to have let the mailman bring in your needs from Djilla, Elaine. I'd have advised it if I'd known your plans.'

There was positively no one like Jackson for advice, Reya thought cynically as E. answered lightly, 'Oh, it was sheer vanity, Jackson. It was an excuse to have my hair done. Tom would have told you our plans yesterday, but you didn't come over . . . Now tell me, will you stay to dinner with us? We'd like it very much.'

Jackson said he would stay, and E. disappeared to the kitchen; Reya disappeared too—to help her and to get away from Jackson.

Later, when dinner was over, she excused herself and went to her room. She had no intention of hanging around in Jackson's company, and she wrote a letter to her father and Hope, and another one to Jean—and included a half humorous reference to 'your heart-throb of a few years ago. He's not married yet, would you believe, but Marlene's back on the scene, so we shall see.' Her letters written, she showered, got into bed, looked through one of the magazines she had bought and then switched off her reading light. She hadn't heard Jackson's car and was wondering how long he would be staying when a shadow appeared in the verandah doorway, black against what she could see of the sky where a huge moon had floated up from the plains and washed the world with soft and limpid light.

'*No!*' said her startled heart as she sat upright, her pulses hammering, and instinctively switched on the bedside light.

It was, of course, Jackson Brand.

Reya blinked in the light. 'What do you want?'

His eyes looked at her darkly and she felt a touch of panic. How dared he intrude on her here, like this?

'You didn't say goodnight before you disappeared,' he said.

She thought, 'This is ludicrous!' Her heart had begun to pound hard against her ribs, and she stammered out, 'I didn't think it mattered. You—you didn't come here to see *me*.'

'That's true.' He crossed the room without hesitation and sat on the side of her bed, then leaned across her, his arm brushing her bosom so that she flinched, and switched off the lamp, leaving them with only the moonlight.

'Why were you driving this evening? Are you trying to make yourself indispensable? What happened to your uncle?'

She swallowed down her annoyance. 'I was trying to make myself useful. My uncle was tired and so was E.' She didn't mention that Tom had had one or two beers too many with his mates, and like Jackson, she kept her voice low. It was unnerving being in the darkness with him, unable to read the expression on his face or to see the stunning blue of his eyes.

'Then don't make yourself *too* useful,' he said warningly. Or was it threateningly? If Reya could have seen him, she might have known. He added unexpectedly, 'Did you invite Warren Livingston-Lowe to come here?'

She hadn't, of course, and yet she didn't want to say so. It might be—revealing. She was, she reflected wryly, becoming a very devious girl. She was developing in some peculiar way a rather large-sized secret life.

When she didn't answer, he insisted roughly, 'Well, do you want him to come? Despite the fact that you left Sydney in such a great hurry the other day?'

Still she said nothing. She felt herself transfixed in silence, unable to tell the truth, unable to lie. Unable to say even to herself what she wanted. Somewhere deep inside her she felt she wanted merely to be left alone, to discover her own truth in the silence and loneliness and emptiness of the bush.

Perhaps two minutes went by. Somewhere along the line she ceased to think of Warren or of her own mixed-up reactions to his coming. She was aware of only one thing, and that was that Jackson Brand was sitting on the side of her bed. Though her eyes had become accustomed to the dark, his face was no more than a silhouette, but the vague moonlight seeping through the glass doors fell across the bed where she sat, and she knew that if he turned his head he would be able to see her face. Carefully, she made it blank, ensured that it would tell him nothing. For all she cared, her expression said, he could sit on her bed all night. To her he was no more disturbing than a cat or something.

Then just when the tension had grown unbearable, when Reya felt they had reached some kind of a deadlock, when her nerves had begun to grow taut, he moved, leaning back on his hands so that the lower part of his back was against her thighs. And it was too much. She wanted to jump out of the bed—to run—to escape . . .

He said, 'This isn't the first time you've been alone in a bedroom with a man, is it?'

She thought instantly of that ridiculous night in the Pott's Point bedroom, of waking to find Warren sleeping on the far side of the bed, not touching her. She was intensely aware of the warmth of Jackson's back against her legs, and her throat was dry. He couldn't possibly know——

'Well?' he persisted, his voice low.

'What does it matter to you?' she breathed out. 'At any rate, I didn't ask *you* to come to my room.' Then swift as lightning she leapt out of bed in her brief cotton pyjamas and made a dash for the inner door. Jackson's arms were clasped around her chest before she made it, and she lowered her head and sank her teeth into the hard flesh of his forearm. He didn't let her go. His only reaction was to pull her closer to him till her back was curved against the hardness of his body. Helpless, tensing, she thought, 'Oh God, he's made of steel——' and she bit him again, desperately.

80

This time he did react. His fingers went to her throat and in a moment she was half choking and ready to beg for mercy. She could hear her own gasps, and could feel her heart pounding as she struggled against him. She knew very well that his passion was aroused, and she felt both frightened and excited, balanced terrifyingly between letting go altogether, agreeing to anything he wanted, and screaming at the top of her lungs so that her uncle would come.

A split second was enough for her to settle for screaming, but as if he knew, one hand covered her open mouth briefly and the next instant he had let her go and disappeared from the room as silently as a shadow.

Reya leaned against the wall to regain her breath. She didn't know if she wanted to laugh or cry or scream—or to run on to the verandah and shout some accusation after him. It was the thought of her uncle and aunt that stopped her from doing that. There was no point in arousing them now. Where were they, anyhow, that Jackson should have the opportunity to come to her bedroom and—and molest her?

He hadn't molested her, of course—except that in the morning when she looked in the mirror there were bruises on her throat where his fingers had pressed into the flesh— bruises that she had to cover from her aunt's eyes with a high-necked shirt.

CHAPTER FIVE

PERHAPS fortunately that day she had little time to brood over what had happened the night before. Tom had gone out early, for there was another mob of wethers to be dipped, and Reya and E. spent most of the day in the kitchen, getting food for the wedding underway. Reya even forgot her bruised throat and unbuttoned the neck of her blouse in the heat of the kitchen with its big old-fashioned fuel stove, but E. didn't see the marks. And that night when Reya went to bed she was too tired to spare more than a fleeting thought for Jackson Brand.

That was when she looked in the mirror and her eyes were drawn to her throat. Exactly what had happened last night? she wondered, meeting her own wide dark eyes in the glass. Why had Jackson come to her room? He had warned her not to try to make herself indispensable, and then he had asked about Warren. After that, somehow she had become too acutely aware of him and they had finished up wrestling together in the darkness. What on earth would E. say if she knew about that? But she would never know. Reya knew she would never breathe a word about it to anyone. In fact, she would put it right to the back of her mind and in future she would avoid Jackson Brand assiduously.

The following morning, she and E. packed up cold meats, poultry, sauces and pastries and desserts into large cartons, and after a scrappy lunch—and with Reya at the wheel because E. admitted to tiredness, and as well to not being over-fond of driving—they set forth for Lilli-Pilli. Reya had never visited the Ramseys' home before, and discovered the white-painted, green-roofed homestead to be large and modern and imposing in its well kept and extensive garden. All around it there appeared to be a beautiful open park— the result of the recent good rains—and she caught her breath. No wonder Marlene had come back to such a home!

But today Marlene was nowhere about, there was only Trisha Ramsey, red-haired like her cousin from Djilla, sitting on the verandah looking very picturesque with a Siamese cat on her lap and a box of chocolates on the table nearby. She was a statuesque young woman of thirty or so, with beautiful skin and hair, and eyes that were a little vacuous. For a moment Reya found herself sympathising with Marlene.

Trisha's expression brightened as E. came along the verandah with businesslike tread, her arms laden with cartons, as were Reya's.

'Trish, we simply must put this stuff in your fridge. We don't have the space at Coolabah . . . This is my niece, Reya Barberton—Reya, Mrs Ramsey—Trisha. May we go through the house?'

The kitchen was enormous and very modern, and off it there opened another large room where there were two vast refrigerators and an even more vast freezer—plus ample cupboards and long shining counters that would be ideal for preparing and arranging foods for a multitude of guests. Under the windows, that looked through a thicket of flowering oleanders, was a big double sink.

Trisha stood by and watched as E., aided by Reya, stored away the food. Then E. stood with her hands on her hips and eyes narrowed, looking around her.

'Where's Jessie, Trish?'

'In her room having a nap. She always does in the afternoons.'

'I'll see her before we go, if I may . . . Now I'll tell you what I thought, dear—we'll use those trestle tables that are stacked in the garage. There are some lovely lacy cloths we can use—old Mrs Ramsey crocheted them herself when she was a bride, I believe. Jessie will know where they are. And I think the sitting room and the verandah outside it will be the best place. It's a pity we can't eat outside and make it a completely outdoor wedding, isn't it? But there are always so many bothersome flies, that's the worst of

Australia.' She rambled on and Reya ceased to listen for a while until E. asked briskly, 'How about overnight guests, Trisha? Can I help in any way?'

Trisha shrugged, then shook her head. 'Nearly everyone's coming by charter plane. Mr and Mrs Lane have arranged it all, he has something to do with the air company, and they're very wealthy people. Otherwise there's only you and Jackson Brand and Milton Lane.'

'The jackeroo from Big Sky?' E. looked curious.

'Yes—well, he's the bridegroom's cousin,' Trisha explained.

'I see. Well, it's all very exciting, dear—guests dropping down from the sky with the minimum of bother and fuss— and disappearing as painlessly. It does make it all much simpler.'

Presently E. went to find the housekeeper, and Trisha made a pot of tea and carried a tray out to the verandah, where she proceeded to pour it so clumsily that Reya longed to snatch the teapot from her and do it herself. Yes, she did have some sympathy with Marlene—however little she liked her. Trisha Ramsey definitely gave an impression of being a useless misfit.

As they drove back to Coolabah Creek, E. remarked with a sigh, 'Poor Trish! She hasn't a clue how to organise even a dinner party for six. I don't really think she's very happy here—there's just nothing for her to occupy herself with. Unless you're born to the outback,' she concluded, 'it's not easy to adapt, no matter what your background or even your natural endowments.'

Was that, Reya wondered as she negotiated a stock grid, a remark made for her benefit—perhaps on Jackson Brand's instructions? Deliberately, she said, 'I guess I must take after you, Aunt E.—I have an affinity for the outback.'

'That will melt away when summer comes,' E. said lightly, and proceeded to wonder aloud when Warren would arrive.

Reya thought she had been answered.

The wedding proceeded according to plan. The whole day in

fact appeared to be a great success, and the only problem that confronted Reya was that of encountering Jackson again. She dreaded that, though she knew it couldn't be avoided.

It was a morning wedding. Susan Ramsey had arrived the day before, and the charter plane was due to land on the Lilli-Pilli airstrip at eleven-thirty. The guests from neighbouring stations had been requested to come earlier as cars would be needed to transport the city people the two or three kilometres from the landing ground to the homestead. To Reya there was something exciting about it all. Trisha looked calm and composed and almost regal in champagne-coloured silk, Marlene, helping the bride, who did not appear till later, was striking in blue, and E.'s hair, Reya thought, looked absolutely gorgeous. Reya had added a chiffon scarf to her own outfit, and hoped that no one would wonder why, seeing the day was sunny and distinctly hot.

As for Jackson, he was already there as she stepped out of her uncle's car, and no matter what her feelings about him, Reya had to admit that he looked devastating in a light-coloured tropical suit that contrasted with his very dark good looks and his wildly curling black hair. She murmured a hardly audible greeting to him as she passed him in the garden on her way to the homestead, and refused to meet his eye. She felt uncomfortable at the very thought of what had happened the other night—it seemed, in strong sunshine under a cloudless sky, utterly incredible.

Fortunately for her, he and Tom and a tall rangy laconic-looking young man, introduced to her as Milton Lane, took off almost immediately in their cars for the station airstrip. Jerry Ramsey drove off too, followed by another of the Lilli-Pilli cars driven by one of his employees. The women went into the house, and E. made a quick check of the kitchen before she sought out the verandah where the lace-covered trestle tables were impressive with silver and crystal.

Later, many complimentary remarks were passed about country hospitality, and Reya was sure that all the city guests believed that Trisha Ramsey had done all the work herself—an illusion that was encouraged by E., and even by Marlene—for the sake of the family honour, no doubt.

A simple and moving ceremony, presided over by the bridegroom's uncle who had come in the charter plane, was conducted in the garden, and this was followed by the wedding breakfast. Marlene was seated, Reya noted almost immediately, between Jackson and Milton Lane, the jackeroo from Big Sky, while Reya, near the end of one of the tables —an unimportant guest—had as her companions the captain and the co-pilot of the plane. She found this a very agreeable arrangement and enjoyed herself vastly talking to both these young men, though her glance strayed now and again to Jackson Brand. She found herself thoughtful over his suavity, his sophistication. To look at him, one would never think he could lose control of himself as he had the other night. She could hardly believe that she herself had sunk her teeth into his forearm, and she shivered slightly at the recollection.

Well, it had all been meaningless. And she might have thought she had imagined it all but for the marks on her throat.

After the toasts were over and the appetites of the guests fully satisfied, everyone began to circulate and to talk, much enlivened by the French champagne that Jerry Ramsey had provided. Reya found herself isolated for a moment with Marlene, who remarked with a pleasant smile that would have deceived any onlookers, 'I can't help wondering about those marks I keep glimpsing on your otherwise very pretty throat, Reya. They're not love bites—I don't think. So what are they?'

Reya went a painful scarlet, and chose rather wildly to be innocent. Eyes blank, she asked, 'What marks?'

Meeting Marlene's eyes directly, however, she had a stultifying feeling that the other girl *knew* what the marks were and, moreover, who had made them. Which would indicate exactly what about Jackson Brand? That he was in the habit of getting himself into such situations with women?

86

Trying not to think about it, Reya moved away from Marlene and sought out the co-pilot again.

It wasn't till some time later when almost everyone was in the garden and the bride had gone to change into her going away dress that Jackson Brand spoke to Reya. She had imagined she was going to escape him, but that would have been altogether too fortuitous. She was loitering alone under a wilga tree in whose delicate flower sprays bees were humming when he came towards her so casually she wasn't certain until the last moment that he had even seen her. But he had seen her—most definitely. He held a half empty, stemmed glass in his hand and the crystal looked unutterably fragile against his dark male strength.

He stopped near her and looked at her quizzically and searchingly, and once again the memory of the other night floated back to her, like a lily on a pond—as real, as vibrant, as transfixing—and she blushed even more deeply than she had when Marlene had spoken to her. Her fingers moved blindly to her throat to ensure that the chiffon scarf was hiding her throat, and his eyes followed the movement of her hand. 'You did that,' her thoughts accused him, though at the same time she wanted to disclaim that he was responsible.

He said in a low voice, 'You shouldn't have run away, you know, honey. Man is naturally a hunter. If you'd stayed in bed where you were, you'd have been perfectly safe.'

Now she felt her cheeks pale and she let go of her scarf. 'It's—it's nothing,' she said huskily.

His dark brows peaked and the corners of his mouth curled. 'Nothing? Then why the scarf? Or do you mean you're used to having bruise marks from a man's fingers on your white throat?' She didn't answer, and he added darkly, 'It might have been more discreet to wear something with a high neckline.'

'Thank you for the advice, but my wardrobe's limited. I'm not as—as affluent as your friends,' she said with a touch of spirit.

'Susie's friends,' he said almost absently. Then, 'It's a

pity Warren Livingston-Lowe couldn't have made it to the wedding. I don't like to see such a pretty girl without an escort.'

'I'm quite happy with things as they are,' she said, and added smartly, 'I certainly don't want *you* to feel obliged to fill in the gap.'

'I wouldn't think of it,' he said blandly—and immediately moved away.

She was left quivering—and suddenly wishing that the whole social occasion would come to an end. She had had enough. She wanted to go back to Coolabah Creek—to days and days of seeing nothing of Jackson Brand. That brief encounter had thrown her. She would so much sooner he had left her alone. Of course he had managed to put the blame on her for what had happened in her bedroom— where he had had absolutely no right to come. She remembered what Warren had said in Sydney—'He'd take what he wanted—he wouldn't spare you——' Perhaps the sub-conscious memory of that was why she had made that dash for safety—was why she had bitten him, she, Reya Barberton, who was not that kind of girl at all.

Finally, it was all over. The bride and groom left in the plane with the city guests, and suddenly the homestead was almost deserted. Marlene had disappeared, and Reya wondered if she was organising the women who were clearing up, but somehow thought it unlikely. E. was tired and looked quite grey, and Tom decided they would go. Good-byes had been said and Reya had settled herself in the car when Jackson came across.

'You did a great job with the breakfast, E.,' he said, and flicked a lazy glance over Reya, but refrained from including her in his congratulations.

E. smiled and Tom said breezily, 'She had a good little offsider in Reya here. Well, E. and I shan't ever have to turn on such a do. No children and we're not well endowed with relatives—a couple of nephews on my side and Reya on E.'s.'

'You might yet have to turn on a do for Reya,' said Jackson with a sardonic gleam in his blue eyes. He leaned indolently against the car. 'A man doesn't follow a girl out to the wild west for nothing.' His eyes tormented her and it seemed to her they lingered on her throat and she only just managed to force herself to leave her scarf alone.

'Well, darling?' E. looked round fondly from the front seat of the car where Tom had settled her.

'Aunt, I am not even engaged,' Reya said, inwardly furious. Across the gravel she saw Marlene and Milton appear, both of them carrying luggage which they proceeded to load into Jackson's station wagon. So where was Marlene off to? she wondered. Western Australia? Nothing had been said about it.

'By the way,' she heard Tom remark, 'Jerry tells me he's thinking of putting in a manager here, and shifting over to the Gold Coast.'

'I thought that would happen,' said E. at once. 'What a shame he didn't have a son. It's always sad to see these big properties pass out of the hands of a family that's held them for generations.'

Was she thinking of Coolabah Creek too? Reya wondered. And did that glint in Jackson's eye insinuate that she, Reya, was ready and willing to hook her little claws in, if she could? Well, she was aware now that Tom had nephews——

But Jackson didn't make even a veiled crack. He said lightly, 'Marlene's still a good country girl. There's no law against a woman's taking over the running of a place—and in my opinion, she'd be quite capable of it, with a little guidance.'

'Poor Marlene,' said E. 'She's having a difficult time. I'm glad she's going over to you for a while. Everlie will appreciate some help just now.'

Reya's heart moved uncomfortably in her breast. So that was where Marlene was off to! She wondered why she found the thought so unpleasant.

A few moments later, Jackson crossed over to his car, and the Westwoods were on their way home. E. talked about the wedding, the bride's gown, the refreshments, and then by some apparently logical route, reached the subject of Jerry's shifting to the coast.

'Of course it's to be understood. Trisha's given it a fair trial, and she'll never fit in here, never be happy.'

'*I* can't understand it,' Tom said. 'Trisha's not a city girl. And look at you—you fitted in here like a penny falling into a slot. So what's wrong with Trisha? And why the Gold Coast, of all places?'

E. paused for thought, then said slowly, 'It's a great thing in the life of a girl like Trisha to have married Jerry Ramsey—a man who can give her the world. And you can't deny she's not getting a very full taste of it at Lilli-Pilli.'

Tom shrugged. 'There are plenty of good things to be enjoyed in the outback. What do you think, Reya?' he tossed over his shoulder. 'Do you find our country style life dull?'

'Not in the least,' Reya began, but E. took over forcefully, 'Reya's here for a holiday, which is a completely different matter. At all events, I think it's a wise move on Jerry's part. He's reached the stage of his life where personal relations are very important. If only Marlene could marry suitably, Lilli-Pilli could continue in the Ramseys' hands even if it's through the distaff side.'

'Who did you have in mind?' Tom asked, amused. 'I rather thought she was doing very well for herself with both Milton Lane and with Jackson. But Jackson of course is a confirmed bachelor.'

'Don't you believe it,' E. said. 'Nature didn't intend a healthy intelligent hunk of masculinity like Jackson to go through life without a wife and without progeny. No, it's going to happen sooner or later, believe me.'

Better luck next time, then, thought Reya rather cattily, thinking she would be glad to reach home and relax.

Warren rang through to the homestead the next morning. Reya heard the telephone through the mists of sleep and five minutes later her aunt came to her door and looked in.

'Oh, you're awake, darling. I didn't call you. That was

Warren on the telephone—a trunk line call. He's bought a car and is on his way out to see us. Rather venturesome of him, but it's certainly the way to see the country ... He's going to let us know when he reaches Djilla or thereabouts. Aren't you pleased?'

Reya didn't know that she was. She wished rather uncomfortably that Warren would leave her alone—at least when it came to making a film star of her! She supposed he would be wanting her to come to Sydney to do a test, and the very thought of that put her right off. Still, there was no certainty that she would be spending the rest of her life here, so she had better consider every alternative. Meanwhile, she merely smiled at E., who went on brightly, 'I assured him he was welcome to stay here just as long as he likes. You'll be able to go picnicking together—I'm sure Tom will let you take the mini-moke.'

Nearly two days passed before they heard from Warren again, and Reya spent those two days restlessly, finding she was able to concentrate on nothing. E. appeared still to be tired after the wedding, and Reya helped her in the homestead and watered the garden in the evenings. She still found time to ride over the paddocks and watch the men mustering the lambs and ewes for the lamb marking, and she wondered as she rode what Marlene was doing over at Big Sky. Was she helping Everlie? Or was she out with Jackson or Milton or both of them? Lucky girl, to have the company of two handsome men, Reya thought wryly. Well, soon she herself would have Warren's company—whether she wanted it or not.

She had the feeling he was going to try to get her away from Coolabah Creek, but she was quite determined to stand her ground. She would not go until she was ready, and just when that would be she didn't know. She had come here so expectantly, hoping in her heart for some kind of fulfilment—some confirmation of the truth of what had lain in her heart all the while she had been away. 'Here is my home, here is where I belong.' Yet no one else thought that way—not even E., apparently, who four years ago had been eager enough to ask Reya to share her home.

Warren was due to arrive at Coolabah Creek some time in the late afternoon, and with E.'s permission, Reya took the mini-moke and drove off to meet him. She had still seen no sign of him when she entered one of the Big Sky paddocks, and there she encountered Marlene and Milton on motor bikes, each with a sheepdog in a box on the back.

'Off to meet your boy-friend?' Marlene asked quite gaily. Reya agreed that she was—it seemed easiest not to dispute the boy-friend bit—and that was the end of the conversation. She continued on her way in the moke, interested to discover that going back to Djilla was oddly different from coming the other way—everything looked different seen from another point of the compass. All the same, she felt fairly confident, and it was great to be out on her own—challenging the outback as it were, discovering whether it was hostile or friendly to her.

She was so wrapped up in recognising turn-offs that she didn't realise how far she had come without encountering Warren until the sun began to disappear. With a feeling of faint alarm, she began to wonder whether Warren had missed the way—or whether she herself had done just that. She pulled up on a narrow bumpy track that was no more than wheel marks and sat quite still looking about her. The sky had faded to colourless and against its pallor some dragonflies chased each other. A sudden burst of sound came from cicadas in a group of trees on her left, one star shone fiercely in the eastern sky, and when she glanced back over her right shoulder, she was dazzled by the singing silver-green of the western sky. Sheep in a paddock over the fence moved slowly, and beyond, the waters of a tank glittered. Reya assured herself that the particular tank was familiar to her—recognisable by a grotesque tree growing nearby—a tree with a silhouette like a great gaunt figure with arms flung out in a weird spirit-dance. But didn't many of the ancient gum trees and eucalypts compel one's imagination with their resemblance to distorted human figures?

Soon it would be dark. So what should she do? Continue to look for Warren? Or would it be wiser to turn the moke around and go back to Coolabah Creek? So long as, in the dark, she didn't get lost . . .

She had not very happily decided on the second course when she discovered a car was coming along the road behind her. Her first illogical reaction was that it must be Warren, and then she realised it was Jackson Brand's station wagon that was pulling up beside the moke. He slid across the seat and leaned out the window and his eyes seemed to scorch her face. A pulse beat fast at Reya's temple. That dark-faced man glared at her with such hostility! And to think she had once made a hero of him!

He said coldly, 'Are you trying to get yourself lost, driving out here after someone who's probably miles off course?'

She swallowed hard. She was really relieved that he had turned up, because she didn't feel all that confident of driving about in the dark. She didn't feel she was yet on good enough terms with this strange, aloof, beckoning land that could be cruel despite its surface graciousness and innocence. But she told Jackson unconcernedly, 'I'm not going to get lost. I know exactly where I am. I've been moving right along the dotted line.'

He smiled sardonically. 'Up until now,' he agreed. 'But if you were my responsibility, I wouldn't like to see you continuing on in the dark. You'd better get out of that moke and come along with me.'

She began to obey, then stopped herself. 'Where to?'

He raised his eyebrows. 'Where would you think? To hunt up your mate—though he deserves to be left out all night, in my opinion.'

'I suppose I deserve that too—in your opinion,' Reya retorted, red-cheeked, as she climbed over the side of the moke. He had opened the car door for her and she slid in beside him and pulled it shut. Jackson's eyes checked over her. She was smart in white pants, a red top with tiny sleeves and a red and white spotted headband, and he took all that in, then let his eyes rest an extra moment on her throat, and on the paling greenish bruises that she had concealed almost perfectly with make-up. She felt her breast rise and fall as her breathing quickened.

'You're all dolled up, aren't you?' he drawled.

'Am I?'

'I'd say so. But then I'm not a city guy ... That dress you have with Love printed all over it—I haven't seen you in that lately.'

'You haven't seen *me* lately,' she retorted. 'Not since the wedding.'

'Missing me?' he asked dryly, and she wished furiously that she had kept quiet. He cast her a mocking glance and those incredibly blue eyes of his unnerved her. There was something disconcerting in the simple fact of their pure blueness—they just didn't match up with the ruthless masculinity of his face. And that was the *sole* reason why they fascinated her. She was willing to bet they had fascinated more girls than you could poke a stick at. The wonder was that he'd never married. Had he been crazy about Marlene to have stayed single all this time? She'd dearly love to know if there was going to be a happy ending to the romance this time and she itched to ask him, to put an end to her own speculation.

Meanwhile, they were speeding along the track, and presently he turned the car sharply, and she commented instantly, 'This isn't the right way.'

'You've got your wits about you,' he said admiringly—though she suspected it was mock admiration. 'You're quite right—this isn't the way to Djilla, but it's the way Livingston-Lowe has taken. In effect, it's at this point he lost contact with whatever directions I must presume him to have been given. I just hope we don't have to track him all the way to——'

'Tibooburra?' Reya suggested, and he laughed outright.

'Where did you get hold of that one?'

'Oh, I get around,' she said, aware that she had liked the sound of his laughter, that it had done something warming

94

to her. It was so nearly dark that she couldn't think how Jackson knew Warren had gone this way, but she was quite prepared to believe that he did, remembering how he had tracked that stockman's child all those years ago.

He kept the car travelling fairly fast, lit one of his inevitable cigarettes, and remained silent. Reya didn't know how many miles they had gone, heading straight for nowhere, judging by the emptiness of the plains stretching all around them and the vastness of a dark sky lit now by star spangles, when what they were looking for came into their sight. A stranded car, just over one of those rises so long and gentle you didn't even know the earth was billowing. A stand of trees extended low and twisting and ghostly and disappeared in the darkness, and the car—Warren's car— lurched like a drunken shadow at an angle to the post and wire fence.

Jackson had slowed down considerably and in the light of his headlamps, Reya saw someone emerge from the other car. It was Warren, of course, recognisable in his violet shirt.

'Got him,' said the man beside her. 'Happy?'

She didn't say anything. She was aware of a peculiar sensation somewhere in the region of her stomach. Seeing how she had flirted with Warren on the ship it should more nearly have been her heart. But quite definitely it was her stomach. Aunt E. would have been disappointed.

Warren, having emerged from the car, stood leaning against it in a leisurely way, took out a cigarette—one of those clove-scented ones, no doubt—and lit up. Jackson said nothing, but she could feel him thinking a lot. She could feel him—every inch of him—emanating contempt for Warren and his whole life style. The word effete came into her mind as they drew nearer. She felt oddly ambivalent. One side of her nature wanted to defend Warren, the other part saw him as Jackson must. But Jackson knew nothing about Warren. *She* knew that he was intelligent, successful and dedicated to his work. Even if Jackson hadn't heard of it, he had made a name for himself.

By now they had covered the distance that separated them from Warren, and the station wagon pulled up behind the car, headlights blazing. It was only then that Reya caught sight of the mangled kangaroo lying on the track. She felt shock, pity, felt her stomach heave, and looked away, her face ashen. Legs shaking, she followed Jackson out of the car. She couldn't look at the dead kangaroo again, and for a second she thought she was going to pass out. That bloody, inert mass—Warren came and kissed her and she was hardly conscious of him, hardly knew that she leaned against him as he put his arms around her. She didn't know what the two men said to each other, she merely heard the murmur of words, and then, blessedly, her faintness passed and she began to be aware of what was going on.

'He came flying across the track in front of me,' Warren said almost conversationally. 'I didn't have a hope of missing him—I'd swerved hard to avoid his mate. Now I've got a flat and as well, I've done in something on the vehicle. I bounced off the fence, you see.'

'Bad luck,' said Jackson crisply. He didn't bother to inspect the car—an expensive-looking red model with sleek lines. Instead he moved over to where the kangaroo lay and stopped to examine it, and at once Reya, who had watched him, felt nausea rise in her again. She had never been able to stand the sight of blood—it was shaming, but it was a fact. 'He's certainly dead,' Jackson said, coming back to the others. 'We'll forget about your car for tonight —I'll send my mechanic out first thing in the morning to take a look at it. You can come back with me.'

Reya walked away blindly and somehow got herself into the back of the station wagon, sinking into the seat and feeling the clamminess of sweat on her brow and neck. She leaned back and closed her eyes and felt enormous relief when Warren took the seat in front beside Jackson. A dead kangaroo—well, a mangled kangaroo—and she was whacked. She hoped Jackson hadn't noticed her reaction ... Now he swung the car around and they headed back the way they had come. The men talked, but she didn't try to hear what they were saying. All she was interested in was pulling herself together. Marlene, she reflected unexpectedly, would have looked over that kangaroo—would have known if it was the male or the female—would have known how it all happened.

Presently her stomach settled down, her sweat dried out, but she was still feeling limp when at last they pulled up at the homestead. But it was Big Sky and not Coolabah Creek, and it was Marlene Newell who came down the verandah steps and not E. Warren got out and Jackson came round the car and opened the door for Reya, taking her arm with fingers that felt like steel, as he helped her out. His blue eyes looked her over in the light that fell from the house and he told her, 'I'm sorry—you're not home yet. I just wanted to let them know what's going on.'

She murmured some answer and tried to keep in his shadow as he introduced Warren to Marlene and then to Milton Lane, who had materialised from somewhere. They all went into the verandah, someone had brought a tray of drinks and Reya sipped from the glass that Jackson handed her. It was something fiery, and she put it down quickly.

'Drink it up,' said Jackson in her ear. 'You look like death—you can't go home to your aunt like that. What's upset you? A dead kangaroo?'

She gulped down the whisky and nodded, feeling tears sting her eyes. She supposed he must despise her for her weakness, but she didn't try to explain. He could think what he liked—think her merely sentimental, anything at all.

When they went back to the station wagon, after Jackson had rung through to Coolabah Creek, Marlene came too and shared the front seat with Jackson, and in the back, Warren put his arm around Reya and drew her against his shoulder.

'God, am I glad to be here! I was getting hungry enough to consider lighting a fire and carving myself a kangaroo steak.'

Marlene laughed. 'But not hungry enough to realise that

you didn't have a knife that would do the job.'

'No, not hungry enough for that,' he admitted. 'Somehow, I thought I might be rescued before I starved to death —since you knew I was coming, Reya, and wouldn't be able to sleep comfortably thinking of me stranded in the middle of nowhere.'

'Reya would never have found you,' said Marlene brightly. 'It was lucky I happened to tell Jackson that she'd gone driving off into the unknown all by herself. What one will do for love! Then we checked with the Westwoods that you hadn't turned up and Jackson decided to take a hand. Travellers who don't know the country can still get lost and die out here, you know. It's not a place you can play games with—and you can't take rescue for granted.'

'If you're subtly suggesting that I'm a heedless, brainless traveller,' said Warren smoothly, 'then I'd like to put in a word for myself. I did my homework on the outback— I've got extra water and petrol and spares, and a good tool kit. It's by no means the first time I've left civilisation to dabble a toe in the wilderness.'

'Really?' said Marlene coldly. 'So how would you have coped if no one had come?'

There was a little silence. Reya was uncomfortably aware of friction, of Marlene making a pretty obvious effort to ally herself with Jackson—who was remarkably silent —against the two outsiders in the back seat.

'You just stayed where you were, didn't you?' Marlene insisted. 'And waited for the deus ex machina.'

'Which came,' he reminded her. 'You can't persuade me I was in any real danger, I'm afraid. I wasn't out in the middle of the desert with no water and a scorching sun beating down on my bare head. I was only a few miles off course, moreover—and I was expected.'

Reya, although she longed to put in a word for Warren, stayed silent, and so did Jackson, and after a second Marlene said sceptically, 'So you stayed in your car and smoked a cigarette.'

'Actually, no. Before it was dark I took some film of the

doe kangaroo, and of a few hundred cockatoos that came to roost in the trees.'

'So you're an amateur film-maker as well, are you?' said Marlene.

'As well as what?' She didn't answer. 'No, I'm not exactly an amateur film-maker. I'm very interested and it happens to tie in with my work. Also,' he continued, when Marlene failed to comment, 'I'm not completely hopeless as a mechanic. If I'd had to sleep out, I'd have changed the tyre and repaired the damage to my car in the morning, and continued on my way.'

'To Tibooburra,' Reya thought, suddenly wanting to giggle. She had the extraordinary feeling that exactly the same thought had occurred to Jackson while those other two were wrangling.

'You sound the complete answer to a maiden's prayer,' said Marlene. 'What do you think, Reya?'

Warren laughed. 'That's not for public consumption, is it, Reya? And as you're the only maiden present, we'll have to leave it there.' Then quickly, before anyone could say anything more, he changed the subject. 'Frankly, Jackson, I'd far sooner have an experienced mechanic fix up my car. I hope it's not too much bother. I'll pay for the work, of course.'

'Oh, I think we can see it through without that,' said Jackson laconically.

Conversation languished from then on until they reached Coolabah Creek. Jackson said they wouldn't come in, and Warren thanked him for coming to the rescue.

'I'd like to hear more about your work some time,' Jackson told him.

'Gladly,' agreed Warren.

In no time the others had gone and Reya was presenting Warren to her aunt and uncle and explaining more fully what had happened. E. was both sympathetic and welcoming, and while she showed Warren to his room, Reya retired to her own for a brush up. Nothing had been said about the mini-moke, but she supposed Jackson would get it back to Coolabah Creek somehow.

In the bathroom, she splashed cold water on her face and decided she looked both exhausted and over-excited. She used rather more make-up than was usual in an effort to hide—something. She hadn't yet sorted out her reactions to Warren's arrival, but one thing she did know, and that was that she was ready to defend him. Because of Marlene, of course. Jackson hadn't been critical as she had expected, and, in fact, he had been positively genial as they had parted.

After dinner—a pleasant meal, with both her aunt and uncle interested in Warren, particularly when they learned that he made television films—she and Warren took a walk around the garden. Nothing had been said yet about his plans for her future, and of that she was glad, but when he stopped with his arm about her and stooped to kiss her lightly by some oleander trees, she had a feeling of strangeness, as if it were all part of an outside pattern. Perhaps it was. Perhaps Warren would kiss any girl he hoped to make into the female lead in one of his television productions. On the ship, she hadn't thought that way. But on the ship she hadn't known, till the last few days, what was in his mind. She'd have been less surprised if he'd asked her to marry him. That was how naïve Reya Barberton was! Here, she discovered she couldn't fool herself so easily—here under this sky that seemed even vaster than the sky above them on the ship. Here where their backdrop was the eternal plains that rose and fell so gently you weren't aware of it. The fleeting shadows of clouds moved softly over the ground and far away a fox or a dingo howled. The few weeks on the ship seemed to belong to so far away they were completely unreal.

As they walked on after he had kissed her, Warren asked, 'Has the wedding happened? I rather gather it has——'

'Yes, several days ago.'

'But no honeymoon? That woman is a bitch,' he added without venom.

Reya was at a loss for a second. Then she thought, 'Of course, he meant Marlene!' And of course too she had told him it was Jackson's wedding. She felt an idiot, but she had to put it straight and said awkwardly 'Oh, Jackson and Marlene aren't married. Not yet, anyhow. I—I got things wrong in Sydney. It was the jackeroo's cousin and Susie, Marlene's sister, who were being married.'

'Good lord! Don't ask me to work that one out tonight. I don't envy Jackson Brand at any rate, if he's going to marry that woman.'

She didn't say it was by no means settled. She had said, 'Not yet', without really knowing why, and he had drawn the obvious conclusion.

'However, to get back to us,' Warren pursued, 'have you thought any more of that proposal of mine?'

'Not really,' she said uncomfortably. 'I've never thought of taking up acting. It just seems—impossible.'

'It's not impossible. And I'm determined to have you.' He surprised her then by taking her in his arms and kissing her again, and when she moved uneasily and he let her go, he said half-humorously, 'You can slip out of my arms, but you're not going to slip out of my net. I'm staying here till I've persuaded you to come back to Sydney with me.'

Reya made no answer and they walked slowly on together. She felt quite sure she would never team up with Warren. And yet, despite herself, she almost believed he could make an actress of her if she wanted it. The trouble was, she didn't want it. She wanted only to stay here in the outback and prove—something—to Jackson Brand. Prove what, though? That he had no power over her movements? That he didn't have sole rights to the outback? That he didn't mean a thing to her? Or was it all of that and something more besides?

CHAPTER SIX

THE next morning the mini-moke was back in the yard. E. said someone from Big Sky had brought it over, and there was a message from Jackson that he'd sent a mechanic out to look at Warren's car which would probably be ready to collect by late morning.

'Shall I stay here and help you, Aunt?' Reya asked. She had noticed that E. was looking pale and rather drawn.

'Darling, of course not! It's just not necessary. You go along with Warren. He can't be expected to find his way around the minute he arrives. Don't worry about me. You young people go ahead and enjoy yourselves. I'm sure there's a lot Warren wants to see before he takes you away from us.'

Reya looked at her aunt hopelessly. What a thing to say! Just as if Reya had confessed that she was in love with Warren. Which she was not, handsome though he looked this morning in a blue and white checked shirt and dark blue jeans—an outfit that made him appear, she reflected with slight amusement, like an actor dressed for a part in a film.

They took the moke and drove over to Big Sky, and on the way discovered that the lamb marking was going on in the yards. As well as Milton, Marlene was there, looking like a station hand in a wide-brimmed hat, dark shirt and narrow-legged pants. Jackson emerged from the milling mob of sheep and lambs to ask, 'You looking for your car? Wait five minutes, will you, and I'll be with you. It's still out in the mulga.'

Warren nodded, and got out of the mini-moke taking his cine-camera with him. He pushed his sunglasses up on his forehead and walked over to the sheep yards, and in a minute Reya, who had stayed where she was, heard the

102

camera whirring. He hadn't asked her to go with him, and she hadn't wanted to. She didn't want to be asked to strike attitudes and get into the picture. Marlene could be the star.

The plastic tags they were putting on the lambs' ears were yellow this spring, she noticed. One ear for the wethers and the other ear for the ewe lambs. As at Coolabah Creek, no brand mark was put on the wool, and it was a simple matter with the coloured tags to classify the lambs according to age and sex. She could smell the familiar odour of wool in the hot sunlight. The grass had been flattened down around the yards and there was a thin haze of red dust in the air and the constant maaing and baaing of lambs afraid of losing their mothers and of ewes afraid of losing their lambs. The mob was small—only about four hundred—so there was little danger of that, but the sheep didn't know it and their alarm was automatic and instinctive.

Reya waited for far more than five minutes, because after a short while Jackson joined Warren and the two men stood talking, their backs half turned towards her. Warren had packed up his camera and she saw him take out cigarettes and offer one to Jackson, who refused. Reya smiled inwardly. She couldn't imagine Jackson smoking a clove-scented cigarette! She simply couldn't. The sun shone on Warren's golden-brown hair and he looked elegant and leisured and very self-assured as he leaned against a fence post, one arm stretched along the rail. Jackson, his hat pushed back on his forehead, looked dark and rough and slightly dusty—very much the man from outback. *His* outback.

The two men talked for what seemed an interminable time. Once Jackson turned his head and indicated the minimoke—or was he indicating her, the girl sitting on it? Reya wondered—with a gesture of one hand. She wondered what they were talking about. She was very much out of it all— not interested in sheep or station affairs, she supposed Jackson must think. That brought her mind to Marlene and she watched the other girl for a while, efficient as any practised station hand, working away with Milton and not even sparing a glance for Warren or for Reya, though she knew very well they were there—mere outsiders who'd come to gawp and weren't of any interest in the life of a countrywoman.

When Reya looked away again, Jackson and Warren were coming towards her.

Jackson nodded a casual greeting, and she thought his eyes lingered momentarily on the open neck of her shirt—which revealed nothing.

'Do you know exactly where Warren's car was stranded, Reya?'

She longed to be able to say yes, but it wouldn't be true. 'Not exactly,' she said reluctantly. 'But I could find it—if you explained——'

He sent her a pained look from his too-blue eyes. 'I'd better come along,' he said briefly. Then to Warren—'You can get in the back of the moke. It's clean enough and you won't be unreasonably uncomfortable. Is that okay?'

'Fine,' said Warren. 'You go ahead and do the driving.' All the same, he grimaced as he squeezed behind Reya's seat and crammed himself into the space behind. There was a bit of matting there, but it certainly didn't look dust-free!

Presently they were speeding along the track, then left it to dodge between scattered trees. Handsome merino sheep were feeding in the paddock, heads down, the sun bright on their fleeces. Jackson looked about him as he drove and Warren, in the back, finished smoking his cigarette. Reya caught the scent of it and found it alien after the wattle and eucalyptus perfumes to which her nostrils had become lovingly accustomed.

'How long do you intend saying with us, Warren?' Jackson asked pleasantly after some minutes.

'That rather depends on Reya,' the other man said, his slightly clipped English accent contrasting strongly with Jackson's lazy drawl. Reya bit her lip in vexation at his merely commenting, 'I see,' and adding, 'You've no fixed plans, then.'

'Not in the immediate future. I'm booked up for Queensland at the end of the year and am hoping to take Reya along too. While she's amusing herself here, I might as well be around—as long as her relatives make me welcome, which they have. The country's quite new to me, and of course I'm interested.'

Jackson braked fiercely at a gate, got out and opened it, drove the moke through, got out and closed it. Reya protested, 'I could have done that.' He didn't answer. A kookaburra swooped from a tree and rose again with a small snake in its mouth, and another kookaburra laughed raucously and maniacally. Reya saw it and heard it anew from Warren's angle, as it were, and wondered if Jackson was doing the same.

When they reached Warren's car, Jackson said, 'Stay where you are, Reya. You've no hat and shouldn't be standing about in the sun.' She sat and watched Warren get into his smart red car, switch on the motor and smile his appreciation. Jackson moved back to the moke, saying over his shoulder, 'Follow me and I'll get you back to Big Sky, and from there Reya can take over.'

Reya made a move to get out of the moke, but he told her almost irritably, 'Skip it, Reya—there's no point in hopping from one vehicle to the other. You're not going to come to any harm with me. So long as you behave yourself and don't panic,' he added, flicking her an ironic glance from his blue eyes.

She coloured and set her teeth and stayed where she was, and he got the moke moving.

'So what are *your* plans?' he asked before they'd progressed very far. 'How long do you intend staying around here?'

'For just as long as my relatives make me welcome— which they do,' she said smartly, and saw his lip curl in annoyance. 'I do help my aunt a little, you know, and she appreciates it.'

'Well, don't try and talk yourself into staying for ever. Believe me, once summer's really with us you won't be able to get away fast enough. Your knowledge of the outback is very limited.'

'And you want it to stay that way, don't you?'

One dark eyebrow rose. 'It might be the least painful course in the long run.'

'What does that mean?'

'Whatever you take it to mean.'

'Then that's exactly nothing—and I'm not in a hurry to go. You pushed me out the door four years ago—but for you I could have stayed with Aunt E.——'

'It's a pity you can't be your age and think that out. You've had a good time in the meantime, haven't you? Here, you'd have caused nothing but trouble. But you're stubborn, aren't you? Did you come back merely to prove to me you could have your own way after all? If so—okay, I've taken the point, you've made it well. But when Warren goes, my advice is that you should go with him and get to know him better. He's a nice enough guy, obviously in love with you, and what's more he has an occupation that could afford you an interesting and varied life.'

'Are you trying to set up a marriage bureau?' she asked, colouring angrily, and reflecting that whatever Warren had told Jackson, he had evidently not told him what his plans for Reya were. 'Anyhow, I don't see that my coming back here need have anything to do with you.'

'That's right,' he agreed, and added almost savagely, 'Nevertheless, despite what we both want, we seem to get involved with one another. All I ask is that you have your fill of the outback—give yourself a proper bellyful and get it over quickly. And don't miss other opportunities by lingering.'

With Warren he meant, of course, and though her heart was beating fast, she said on a bored note, 'You certainly harp on the one string, don't you? I wish I'd got out of this vehicle and gone with Warren.'

'Why didn't you, I wonder?' he asked ironically. 'You

don't have to keep doing as I say—as you're so very fond of telling me. So what's the matter? Do I still fascinate you?'

Her heart hammered harder. She said, outraged, 'You *never* fascinated me.'

'No? I'll be more honest and admit that you fascinate me, honey.' He said it grimly and she had no idea how to take it. She waited for him to say something uncomplimentary about *why* she fascinated him—with her stubbornness, her stupidity, something of that sort—but he didn't say it. Jackson's jaw was jutting and his eyes were narrowed. 'You were always the one who drew the eye. Those sisters of yours—they were blonde and pretty and obvious. You were the one with the dreams, the one with the soft and vulnerable mouth, the dark soulful eyes that petitioned so overtly and didn't even know it.' He paused, drove round a tree stump, and added, 'You were the sexy one. Now you're old enough to be married, and marriage is quite obviously what you hanker after. So take care—take care, do you hear me?—who you give your heart to.'

Reya blinked, feeling her nerves strung taut, not quite sure what he was talking about. 'Are you—are you warning me off Warren? A minute ago I thought you were urging that I should disappear with him——' Her voice emerged uneven; it had shocked her to hear him talking the way he had of the girl she had been. Last time—he had referred to her unflatteringly as a skinny schoolgirl.

'I'm talking of anyone you fancy,' he said roughly. 'Anyone at all. Anyone who sets your pulses racing.' He braked at a gate that had to be opened and she swung her legs to the ground.

'Yes, you get it,' he said. 'Then run off back to Warren. We've had enough of each other's company.'

She didn't answer. She opened the gate, didn't look at him as he took the moke through, then waited for Warren. Her nerves felt ragged. Jackson had insisted she stay in the moke—now all he wanted was to be rid of her.

When she had got into Warren's car, he gave her a surprised look. 'What's the matter? You look as if you've been having an argument.'

She shrugged. 'It's just—that man rubs me up the wrong way. He always has. I can't stand him.'

'You're not his type,' Warren said. 'All the same, if I had any say in what you did or didn't do, I wouldn't allow you to spend a single moment alone in his company. There's a little too much of the brute about him.'

Reya didn't comment. She didn't want to spend a moment alone with Jackson. As for him being a brute—she already knew something about that.

A few times during the following days Reya thought of what Jackson had said, and she knew that though she had denied being fascinated by him, it wasn't true. Fascinated was exactly what she was—and she didn't mean that in a complimentary way. It was just something she couldn't help. She couldn't keep her mind from worrying at him, and it had always been that way—when she was here as a schoolgirl, and later when she was back in England. If he wasn't in her conscious thoughts, then he appeared in her dreams, riding that black horse, and she couldn't keep him out.

She tried to persuade herself that the reason for her obsession, at least in the latter part of what you might call their *non*-relationship, was that he was the one who had so heedlessly destroyed her dreams and her hopes—and yes, her delicate fragile emotions. *They* had been bruised and battered out of existence when he had so unfeelingly flung her down on the cane lounger at Big Sky four years ago. As for himself, telling her she fascinated him—painfully she came to the conclusion that all he had meant by that was that he found her—for some reason she couldn't fathom—sexy. It was not a thought that gave her pleasure, because so obviously it was the one and only thing that attracted him to her—that brought out the brute in him. He didn't *like* her—it was just a physical thing, nothing else.

It was something of a relief to get her thoughts straight-

108

ened out even this much, and a still greater relief not to see him. She spent her time with Warren, driving round in the moke or riding around the paddocks. He was a competent enough horseman, but he never looked in the least like anyone else around the place—perhaps not unnaturally. He looked like a gentleman rider.

By now Reya had read part of the script of the film he was to produce—the first episode—and though she found it interesting, she couldn't identify herself with Marie, the semi-sophisticated, wilful daughter of a rich man who fell in love with a drover. Berenice Esmond, she couldn't help thinking, would have fitted the role to perfection, and quite possibly it had been written with her in mind. When it came to reading the lines out aloud, she was hopelessly shy.

They spent one Sunday afternoon down by the creek, which was rapidly drying up, in the cool shade of the tall trees. E. hadn't been feeling too well, so Reya had prepared the lunch, and her aunt had gone to her room to lie down. Now, while Warren swung in the hammock, Reya read some of Marie's lines, her voice sounding so small and insignificant against the great outback silence that she was embarrassed. Quite suddenly, Warren tipped himself out of the hammock, put his arms around her and kissed the tip of her small straight nose.

'You just don't believe in yourself yet, do you? Well, never mind, a little practice will loosen you up and by the time I get you back to Arthur you'll be quite presentable.'

Reya shook her head. 'I'll never be like Berenice Esmond.'

'I wouldn't want you to be,' he said almost sharply, and kissed her again, this time on the lips. 'And no matter what happens, I'll still find a use for you.'

What that meant she didn't have a chance to discover, because someone came towards them through the long shadows of the late afternoon. Reya felt her heart jolt. Jackson Brand coming back into her life. Their eyes met and locked as she stood looking towards him, Warren's arm still

109

around her, the script in its stiff cover on the hammock where Warren had tossed it.

'Sorry if I'm intruding,' Jackson drawled, his eyes releasing her and acknowledging Warren. There was a slight sardonic twist to his lips. 'I'm afraid you'll have to come up to the house.'

Reya flushed, wondering if he had heard their conversation. She somehow didn't want him to know about her non-existent theatrical ambitions. She was so concerned, in fact, over her own personal and peculiarly turbulent feelings that she didn't suspect anything was wrong till Warren asked sharply, 'What's happened?'

In that instant she realised there had been something sombre in the way Jackson had spoken, and she sent him a startled look of sudden alarm.

'Nothing to get upset about,' he said quietly. 'You know Elaine hasn't been well. It's not the first time she's had these pains, but they've become pretty severe. Tom's taking her in to the hospital at Djilla to have another check-up. They'll have to stay the night.'

Reya felt a sick agitation. She felt guilty too that she hadn't realised her aunt was feeling *so* ill. But E. was the type of person who always minimised her own suffering. 'Oh,' she exclaimed, 'I'll go and help her pack. Poor Aunt E.! I shouldn't have left her alone this afternoon.'

'Don't exaggerate,' Jackson said curtly. 'It's not a critical situation, and she wasn't alone. As for the packing, that's been done. Tom didn't know where you two were, so he left it till I came over.'

And Jackson, of course, with his uncanny ability, had tracked them down straight away ... By now they were walking up from the creek bank in the direction of the homestead, Reya moving quickly, a little ahead of the men. She heard Jackson say civilly, 'You two had better come across to Big Sky for a couple of nights.'

'Fine,' said Warren at once. 'It's very good of you to ask us.'

Reya flung back agitatedly over her shoulder, 'There's no

need.' She would talk to her uncle and aunt, she thought. They didn't have to do what Jackson said—and there was something definitely disturbing in the thought of sleeping over at Big Sky.

At the homestead, Tom was already helping E. into the car, and at the sight of her aunt's white, strained face, Reya said nothing of what was on her mind.

'Aunt E., I didn't know you were feeling so bad. You should have told me.'

'It's nothing, darling,' E. said with a bright smile. 'Just a recurrence of some pains I had once before. A few tablets, and I'll be home again. Jackson will look after you while we're away.'

'That's right,' Tom agreed. 'You and Warren get what you need from the house and go over to Big Sky. It's all set —I've talked to Jackson.'

Reya bit back a protest. She didn't think her uncle didn't trust her, but he was a conventional man who liked everything to be done properly, and he wouldn't think it right for her and Warren to be left here, virtually alone. So it looked as if she would have to accept the inevitable and go with a good grace, and hope it would be for only one or two nights.

She wondered later, when they were on their way, if Marlene was still there.

Marlene was. She was playing tennis with Milton in the last of the daylight when the others arrived, Reya and Warren in Warren's car, following Jackson in his station wagon. If Reya had imagined she might possibly be helping Everlie cook the dinner, she was mistaken, and though Marlene waved her racquet in acknowledgment of their arrival she didn't leave the court. It was Jackson who showed them to the bedrooms they were to occupy.

Warren was enthusiastic, interested in the age and subsequent modernisation of the homestead, for while its exterior was almost pioneer style, inside there was every modern convenience. There were even, Reya discovered later, three bathrooms.

She had just finished unpacking the few things she had brought when Jackson said from the doorway, 'May I come in?'

Flushing faintly, she said a stiff, 'Yes.' She had changed into—of all things—her Love dress, and his blue eyes wandered over it with amusement before they came to rest on her face. He said without preamble, 'I just wanted to assure you that it wasn't my idea for you to come to Big Sky.'

She bit her lip. 'That's very hospitable of you,' she said with a sarcasm which he ignored.

'Tom didn't want to leave you alone in the house with Warren—more or less. Your aunt was more concerned that you shouldn't have the bother of household tasks. So this is how we worked it out. You're not to feel yourself obliged to help Everlie. She has the two housegirls to help her and though she's pregnant, she's a country girl and takes it all for granted.'

So that, Reya reflected, accounted for Marlene's enjoying herself on the tennis court while Everlie toiled in the kitchen preparing dinner for—how many people? Seven adults and three children. Quite a task. But of course Everlie, like Marlene but unlike Reya Barberton, was a country girl. Meanwhile Reya Barberton couldn't think of a thing to say and Jackson's blue eyes were looking at her in the most unnerving way, taking in the whole of her—including, she felt very definitely, everything that was hidden by the cotton jersey dress.

All the same, she was completely surprised when he covered the distance between them and pulled her roughly against him. There was dead silence for a moment. Then she heard the heavy thudding of her heart. Or was it his? She raised her face and looked up at him. A pulse was beating visibly at his temple and she watched it for seconds, hypnotised. Then her eyes travelled to his and she seemed to lose her identity in their blue blueness, until, as if drawn by some strong invisible current, she felt herself lean towards him. Their lips touched, briefly, electrically. She felt him tense and she tensed herself and knew she must pull away. She did so, and her own unspoken query hammered at her brain: Why? Why does it happen? Because he found her sexy? Which meant—exactly what? And was she going to be blamed this time? That other time —he'd said, If you'd stayed in bed you'd have been safe . . . They both stood motionless for several seconds, only inches apart. Then she said on a breath, 'What did I do wrong this time?'

His voice as low as hers, and as edgy, he said, 'Nothing, God knows.' And then on a lighter note that was almost flippant, 'It's what you get for teaming up that dress with a pair of ultra-expressive black velvet eyes.'

Reya turned away from him, her lashes coming down instinctively. 'You didn't have to cross the room,' she said indistinctly.

'No, I didn't,' he agreed. She half expected him to make an apology, but he merely added formally, 'We have dinner at eight. That's'—consulting his watch—'in eighteen minutes' time. I'll see you then.'

He went, and Reya walked over to the mirror and sat down in front of it, to comb her dark hair, put on a pale lipstick and a touch of eye-shadow. But mostly to stare at herself as though she were some unrecognisable person. 'Tomorrow afternoon,' she thought, 'Warren and I will go back to Coolabah Creek.' She prayed—though not only for that reason—that E. would be home by then.

Something was quite certainly happening to her, and she didn't want to try to sort out what it was.

Dinner was not exactly a comfortable meal, partly because there were still sparks flying between Warren and Marlene. Marlene continually needled Warren—he was English, he was ignorant, he was in some unspecified way inferior. That was Marlene's opinion of most outsiders, apparently. Warren, on the other hand, was at no pains to hide the fact that he didn't find her an attractive female. There were just the five of them at the table, Milton making the fifth. Everlie and Don and their children ate in their own quarters. Milton appeared blissfully unaware of any undercurrents of hostility. Tennis, the day's work with the sheep, the weather, the good food—these topics seemed to absorb him utterly.

After dinner, Jackson and Marlene played chess and Milton pored over a book on wool fibre improvement. Reya and Warren went through to the verandah. Warren was restless, he liked to be doing something, and presently he insisted they should go for a walk. They went beyond the garden and as far as the shearing shed. They looked inside the long low building that housed the shearer when shearing was on, they poked around the shearing shed with its greasy floor, looking at the big wool presses, at the tables where the fleeces were flung, at the stands with the electric shearers. They looked in fact at everything, and Warren knew more about it than Reya did. She thought Marlene underestimated Warren when she belittled him as some sort of a city slicker. He was far from being that, and the thought made her smile a little. She asked him when they went outside again into the cool night air, 'Why don't you like Marlene, Warren?'

He shrugged. 'She's got an outsize ego—she's too bossy, and I don't like that in a woman. Does it show?'

'It's pretty obvious,' she admitted, and added inconsequently, 'But don't worry, we'll be back at Coolabah Creek soon. I'm sure Aunt E. will be all right.'

They walked slowly back to the homestead. Warren began to quote some lines from *South of the Gulf*, and a little to her own amazement, Reya came in on cue and spoke Marie's lines. In the dark it was so much easier—it was like wearing a mask, and she thought that deep down there must be at least a little of the actress in every woman. It was largely a case of letting go, and it was much easier to let go when you felt yourself invisible—which you certainly wouldn't feel with a movie camera on you and a camera crew ranked around, even out in the middle of nowhere.

Warren put his arm around her. 'Lovely. Perhaps you'll

begin to believe me now when I tell you all things are possible for you.' His kiss was bestowed like a reward, she reflected ironically—it was like giving a dog some titbit for performing a lately learned trick. And if she could regard a kiss like that—well, there was something sadly missing.

They parted company on the verandah. The light was still on in the sitting room and Reya didn't know if Jackson went to join the others or not. She went straight to her room and discovered she was wiping Warren's innocuous kiss from her lips.

After she had undressed and was about to get into bed she crossed the room and locked the door. There were of course two doors, and she locked the verandah door too. She knew very well who she was locking it against, and it wasn't Warren.

She and Warren went out the next day in his car, to see the men and dogs working the sheep. Warren wore a light jacket suit in narrow fawn and white striped cotton cloth, and a smart-looking cotton hat—and of course his sunglasses. They watched the lambs and ewes being yarded ready for more lamb marking, with Marlene taking her part and ignoring once more the city guests. Reya was well aware of being regarded as an outsider, but Warren was too intent on observing to care what anyone thought of him. He even set up his ciné-camera and shot a short sequence or two—'just for the record,' he told Reya with a good-humoured smile. Marlene, workmanlike in blue denim and broad-brimmed hat, was the star—and fully conscious of it. She strolled over afterwards with a superior smile.

'A souvenir of your outback days to take home?'

'You could call it that,' he said equably. 'My thanks to you for a good performance, at any rate.'

Marlene looked at him doubtfully, and Reya said, 'I used to love watching the lamb marking on my uncle's place when I was a schoolgirl.'

Marlene gave her an odd look, and when Warren moved away to talk to one of the men, she remarked, 'I suppose

115

your idea is to impress Warren with the idea that your uncle is a wealthy grazier, is that it?'

Reya raised her eyebrows and flushed faintly. 'I don't know what you're talking about.'

Marlene laughed cynically. 'Oh, don't be thick—you know very well. But don't worry, I shan't give you away. After all, for you it could be vital.' And she too moved away.

Reya went back to Warren's car thoughtfully. The sun was hot, and foolishly she hadn't brought a hat. Jackson, completely absorbed in work, had barely spared a glance for the visitors, though she had been waiting with a kind of nervy anticipation for him to come and speak to her. Sitting in the car, she tried not to look at him, and thought instead of what Marlene had said. Obviously her uncle was not wealthy—and she was well aware that Coolabah Creek was much smaller than Big Sky or Lilli-Pilli. But she hadn't been trying to impress Warren and she couldn't think why Marlene had made such a pointless and petty remark. Not that it mattered.

Jackson still hadn't come over to the car when finally they drove away, and Reya determinedly forgot him and gave all her attention to the countryside. It gave her considerable pleasure to look about her as Warren drove confidently across a seemingly endless paddock. Already the green colour was fading from the grasses, the wild flowers were disappearing, the golden fluff of the wattle blossom was matting and darkening. The dried out, pale colours that she knew best were coming back into the landscape, and this vast paddock was a soft tapestry green, while in contrast the clumps of trees were bluish and blotted like shadows. Above, the sky was pale too, and a few galahs flew across, the rose pink of their breasts and underwings making her catch her breath with a pleasure that was more than half nostalgic remembrance. She thought what pain it would be never to see these things again.

That night after she and Warren had taken a walk in the

garden they went back to the homestead to learn that Tom had rung. Jackson called Reya into the sitting room to tell her the news when she would have gone straight to her bedroom, and reluctantly she followed Warren inside. Tonight Marlene was sitting over the chessboard with Milton and didn't bother to look up as the other two came in.

'Tom has to take your aunt to Sydney, Reya,' Jackson told her almost gently, and she stared at him with widened fearful eyes. 'She's been referred on to a Macquarie Street specialist.'

Marlene raised her head to say coldly, 'I suppose you two will drive down to Sydney.'

'If it's necessary,' said Warren, with an inquiring look at Jackson.

Reya's senses were whirling. Was her aunt seriously ill? Would Uncle Tom want her to come? She too looked at Jackson, who shook his head slightly.

'Your aunt doesn't want you to worry. You'll stay here and we'll see what eventuates. So far, there's absolutely nothing to get upset about. They may even be back in a few days' time.' The corner of his mouth lifted and his blue eyes smiled slightly as he added, 'Meanwhile, this is your one and only home.'

She paled a little and looked away. That smile was rather humourless. She supposed he disliked having her stay here—but for her uncle's sake, he accepted it. Well, she didn't particularly like being here on sufferance, but she did want to be around when E. came back. So here she would stay. She was certainly not going to flee from the outback because of Jackson Brand's antipathy—unless of course Tom wanted her in Sydney. No, even if Jackson made it plain he was not pleased to have her as a guest, she would dig in her toes and she would stay.

At least he was civil—and more than civil—to Warren. In fact, the next day he set himself out to be a good host and to see that Warren became acquainted with everything possible about the running of a big sheep station. No

117

specific invitation was issued to Reya, however, and as Everlie was feeling poorly that day, Jackson had asked Marlene to take over—and see to the children and the cooking. Reya stayed home too, though she didn't think Marlene and she would particularly enjoy each other's company.

Marlene *was* bossy, she discovered. She sent Reya out to the schoolroom to supervise the two older children's correspondence school lessons, and to keep four-year-old Michael entertained, and that took care of the morning.

The men didn't come in to lunch, and it was Reya who prepared a salad for everyone while Marlene saw to it that the children laid the table. Dinner, however, was a joint effort with Reya doing the vegetables and Marlene being creative with casseroled chicken.

Afterwards, Marlene and Warren played chess—a not altogether friendly game, for each of them was determined to win, and Jackson and Milton did some bookwork in the office.

Tom rang late at night. E. was to go into hospital for a gallstone operation and he was going to stay in Sydney. Reya spoke to him and asked him if he would like her to come and stay with him.

'No, my dear, Elaine's in very good hands, and I'm staying at a hotel not too far from the hospital. Jackson will see that everything's all right on the station. You carry on as you are and don't worry—that's E.'s special message for you.'

Reya gave in because there seemed nothing else to do, though it irked her to be beholden to Jackson, who, while assuring her she was welcome to stay, proceeded to ignore her.

She spent the next two days at the homestead, helping Everlie, while the others, Warren included, were out all day. Those two days were the longest she had ever known, and she felt more depressed and blue than she would have believed possible. It wasn't only that she was worrying about her aunt. It was also that for some maddening

118

reason she couldn't stop herself from thinking about
Marlene riding out there with the men—from picturing her
with Jackson . . .

It was a massive relief when Tom rang through with the
news that the operation was over and that E. had come
through it well.

'Everything's fine here, Reya, and E.'s anxious already to
to hear news of you. Is Warren still there?'

'Yes, Uncle. Tell E. that there's nothing to worry about.'

'That's great, keep enjoying yourselves—get Jackson to
show you around. And pass on the news to him, will you?'

Reya did so the moment Jackson came in. Marlene went
straight through the house to shower and change, and
Milton did likewise, while Warren had gone off somewhere
with his camera—to capture the sunset. So there was no
one else about when she sought out Jackson.

She discovered when she confronted him that she was
looking over him searchingly—to find the marks of another
woman on him. It was an extraordinary and ridiculous
idea, but that was exactly what she was doing. As if, in
the sweat and dust that streaked his face, she could discern the touch of another woman's lips. As if, she told
herself, angry with her own stupidity, as if Marlene and
he were in the least likely to have been kissing out there
in the hot sunlight as they rounded up sheep. How idiotic
could you get? And anyhow, suppose they had been kissing
—what did it matter to her?

Yet somehow it did matter, and agony tore at her heart.
What had happened? How had she come to feel this way?
Was it because she had stayed home brooding and alone?
Before, she had thought she would be positively glad if
Marlene and Jackson did get married—and went away on a
long honeymoon. Now she knew that if that happened she
would have to flee. She simply wouldn't be able to stay
here. Or was it only because he was still free that she had
allowed herself to feel this way? Yet she was not even conscious of having allowed it. It had simply taken her unawares.

119

She had set out a tray on the verandah with its cool green tiles and its slanting roof. There were glasses, ice, a decanter of whisky. Jackson tonged out ice cubes, splashed whisky into a glass, then tossed down his drink and looked at her over the empty glass as she stood staring at him.

'Well?'

Her treacherous mind chose that moment to remind her that it was here she had first experienced him physically—that this cane lounger so close to her was the one on to which he had thrust her—She cut the thought off and said coldly, 'My uncle rang. The operation is over and Aunt E. is doing well.'

He smiled, but his eyes were veiled. 'That's great news.' He set down his glass and tilted his eyebrows inquiringly. 'Something else?'

She clenched her fists and unclenched them. She had had enough. 'Yes. I don't think we—Warren and I—will stay here any longer.' She said it not quite steadily.

Jackson smiled faintly and pushed back the dark curling hair from his forehead. 'You don't,' he said flatly. 'Of course it had to happen, but I'd have thought you'd have held out a little longer. You're bored to tears with your little taste of what it means to be an outback housewife. Is that it?'

'Not at all,' she retorted angrily. 'When I said here, I meant right here—in your house.'

His eyes hardened. 'What did your uncle suggest? Now don't tell me any lies—in fact, you needn't tell me anything. I know what Tom wants—and your aunt too. Don't get the idea that I'm begging you to stay, but while you're here you stay at Big Sky. With me. I have a duty towards you while your relatives are absent.' He stroked his chin—he needed a shave—and looked at her levelly, and Reya met his eyes and knew at once that she absolutely shouldn't have done that.

It was as if warm water slid down her spine. It was as if—as if she'd received just enough of a tingling electric shock to make her legs give way under her. Her heart palpitated and she felt sick—sick the way she had felt that spring long ago when just to look at him, though it was utter bliss, was still a bliss so incomplete that her whole being cried out for more and she was sick for wanting it.

She said stumblingly, 'I can't stay here—it's——' She saw his hand reach out and then, instead of touching hers, Jackson turned half away and took cigarettes from the table.

'Here, have a smoke,' he offered, his voice cool.

Reya took a cigarette with fingers that shook and put it between her lips. The flame of the lighter trembled gauzily as he held it for her and through it his face was dark and shimmering, and his eyes were like blue jewels. She drew smoke into her mouth in an effort to appear practised, though it was only about the fourth time she had ever smoked. Just now it seemed to be a desperately needed distraction, and she thought she coped very well. Which showed, she thought wryly, that Warren was right. She could act—if she really wanted to. Jackson had lit up too and was gazing across the garden, his eyes narrowed. Then his eyes came back to her.

'Relax,' he said softly. 'You've been all tensed up worrying about Elaine. It's all over now.'

She managed a smile, and several seconds went by.

'Do you play chess?' he asked unexpectedly.

She blinked and almost choked on a lungful of smoke. 'No, not really. That is—I've only played once or twice.'

'I'll give you a game tonight,' he decided. 'It will do you good—get your mind quietened down.'

She bit her lip. God knew, her mind needed quietening down—she hoped Jackson didn't realise how much. But she doubted whether a game of chess with *him* would have the required effect.

'And by the way,' he went on, his tone casual, 'when you do leave here, Pott's Point is out. So you'd better start thinking of alternatives now.' Reya felt colour swamp her face and parted her lips to make some protest, but he swept on remorselessly, 'I've had a talk with Warren. He's

121

been quite frank—which you have not—and I know, and *you* know, that your aunt would definitely not approve of your sharing a bedroom with a man—any man—before you're married to him. It may seem old-fashioned to you and Warren, but I can't help that. So have you any ideas of your own as to where you'll billet yourself? Or shall I contact some of my city friends and make arrangements for you?'

Listening to him, she had felt herself go rigid with shock. Warren had talked to him—told him about—*that*! She couldn't believe it. Exactly what had he said? And *why*? She could have died ... Her face white, she stammered out, 'I—I don't want to discuss it with you. It's not your business.'

She had forgotten about her cigarette and she didn't like the taste of smoke anyhow, and her mouth was dry enough. She leaned down to the ashtray, and Jackson caught her by the wrist as she straightened. At his very touch, her nerves screamed. Despite everything, they screamed for him to pull her against him and kiss her. That was unmistakably what they did, and the awareness of it almost drowned her out of consciousness. She was as confused as anyone could ever be—because she simply shouldn't feel this way when he was so utterly aggressive and antagonistic where she was concerned.

He didn't pull her against him and kiss her. But his eyes looked black rather than blue as he asked her flatly, 'Are you going to marry Warren?'

She shook her head wildly. His fingers were scorching her wrist like a flame.

'What does he want of you?'

'Hasn't he—told you?' she asked huskily.

'Suppose *you* tell me.'

Reya took a deep breath. 'He's asked me to play a part in the film series he's going to make. In Queensland,' she added. Even to her own ears, it sounded impossible, and she almost hoped he hadn't heard. But he had, of course.

'Good God,' he said slowly. 'So you have ambitions. You

wanted this when you invited him here.' He let go of her wrist and mashed out his cigarette with a kind of slow violence. She watched him and didn't contradict what he had said. It seemed irrelevant to explain that Warren had followed her out here because it was what *he* wanted. The thing that stunned her was that he took it seriously, when she would rather have expected him to laugh her to scorn.

She was rubbing her wrist without realising it and he commented absently, 'I suppose that will bruise.' His eyes travelled to her eyes, then to her lips and down the whole slender length of her as though assessing her in a new light. Finally he frowned, and said abruptly, 'I'll see you at dinner. I need a shower.'

After dinner, Warren challenged Marlene to a game of chess and soon they were quite grimly competing. Milton, looking not too pleased about it all, found himself some literature on wool growing—he was certainly keen!—and settled in a chair where he could keep half an eye on the play. Jackson had crossed over to a cedar chest that stood against the wall—an old, sheeny piece of furniture that looked as if it had been there a long time and taken good care of—and from it he took an ivory chessboard and a handsome carved wooden box which contained a beautiful set of chessmen.

'These pieces were carved by the first William Jackson Brand to settle in Australia—away back in the days of the squatters, before this part of the country was opened up,' he told Reya as he proceeded to set up the chessboard. He asked her to tell him the name of each piece and what moves it could make, and she concentrated hard and tried to quell her nerves at finding herself so close to him. She was afraid she was going to show up as being very much Marlene's mental inferior—Marlene could do everything! —but as the game progressed, he found Jackson surprisingly tolerant and helpful, and presently she actually relaxed and began to enjoy herself and the challenge to her intelligence.

Meanwhile, Warren for the first time had beaten Marlene

and they both came to watch the other game. Reya kept her equanimity for a short while, but went completely to pieces when Marlene suddenly asked, 'What's happened to your wrist, for heaven's sake? You look as though someone's been strong-arming you.'

Reya went crimson and then pale, and Jackson said blandly, 'I've been strong-arming her, of course. Into brushing up her chess,' he added.

Reya made a hopeless stupid move, and Marlene remarked, 'It looks like a losing battle. Chess isn't everyone's game.'

Warren said, 'She's doing all right,' and Jackson said, 'It's not the only game in the world. We'll have another lesson tomorrow night, Reya, if you've had enough for now.'

Reya had had enough. She surrendered her place to Marlene and thought that was probably what they both wanted. She went on to the verandah and looked at the night—at the sky teeming with stars, and the Milky Way fleeing like a mist across the darkness. It was all incomparably lovely and she couldn't imagine ever again having to live without it. Yet she wished, just a little, that she had never come back to Australia.

Warren hadn't followed her straight away, and when he came she said abruptly, 'I'm tired. I'm going to bed.' And went.

Somehow she didn't feel up to dealing with Warren in any way at all tonight.

CHAPTER SEVEN

WARREN didn't go out with the others the following morning. He had been rather quiet at breakfast, his eyes watchful, and when later, with the three children in tow, Reya headed for the schoolroom, Everlie intercepted her.

'Not today, Reya—please! Warren will screw my neck if I impose on you while he's around. I can manage on my own—I usually do. I'm as fit as a sand turkey. Now you kids let go of Reya and come along with me.'

Reya gave in, and the little procession moved on along the hallway and she went out to the verandah where Warren was sitting.

'What do you want to do?' she asked him, and despite herself her voice was cool as she remembered that he had talked about her to Jackson.

Warren got to his feet and came towards her across the green-tiled floor. 'First I'd like to know what I've already done. You haven't looked me straight in the eye this morning and you barely spoke to me last night.'

She could have reminded him that he had been neglecting *her* more than somewhat, but as it happened she didn't really care about that one way or the other. Instead, she looked at him directly and said, 'I think it was unfair of you to tell Jackson what you did about—about me.' .

He screwed up his eyes. 'What did I tell him about you?'

'Something personal and private,' she said, flushing, certain he must know what she was referring to.

'All right,' he admitted after a second. 'So I said something about Arthur's flat. Well, I apologise—but it was just a subject that came up. How did he happen to mention it to you?'

She shrugged and repeated his own words, ironically. 'It was just a subject that came up.' Then at his own look of annoyance, she added quickly, 'Jackson's—concerned about where I'll stay when I leave here. He feels responsible, with my aunt and uncle away.' It gave her a strange feeling to be defending Jackson Brand as she undoubtedly was, when she herself had practically told him to mind his own business, and now Warren looked more annoyed than ever.

'That would appear to be the whole trouble. He may be a great guy, but he has too much to say where you're concerned for my liking. When he started asking me impertinent questions, I told him what I did to get him straightened out—to underline the fact that he doesn't own you. Marlene what's-her-name is supposed to be his girl-friend, and one at a time is enough, I should have thought.' He paused, then continued, 'By the way, I *haven't* discussed with Jackson Brand the fact that I have hopes of your playing Marie in the Queensland show. I don't want him trying to quash that.'

'He wouldn't, as a matter of fact,' she said dryly. 'I know—because I told him about it yesterday.'

'And what was his comment? That you'd never make an actress?'

Was that what Warren expected? she wondered, and the query followed, Did Warren really believe in her ability? But if not, why was he being so persistent? She told him, 'He didn't comment at all.' She wondered what Warren would think if she told him Jackson Brand had gone out of his way to see she was cleared out of his vicinity four years ago and that, whatever Warren suspected, he hadn't become one little bit more enamoured of her in the meantime.

Warren had come to stand beside her at the verandah rail, and they both looked out at the sunlit garden without speaking. Then, because she simply had to know, she demanded, 'What did you tell him happened that night?'

He looked at her in cool surprise. 'Do you think I'm some sort of louse? I told him the truth—that there was

126

only one bedroom available but that I didn't—take advantage of the fact.'

Reya felt immense relief, yet she wished desperately that he had slept in the lounge or on the floor or—anywhere. It hadn't been fair of him to sleep where he had, and if she hadn't fallen asleep at once, and if she hadn't slept so soundly——

'I didn't go as far as to say I bunked down on the floor,' Warren said, sounding vaguely amused. 'Chivalry's assumed a new image with Women's Liberation and that's common knowledge. I imagine it might even have reached the folk out here in the mulga,' he finished, deliberately, she thought, using the Australian colloquialism to dispel an over-serious atmosphere that had crept into the conversation. 'Now am I forgiven?' He put his arm around her, and reluctantly, Reya allowed it to stay there. 'The last thing I want is to leave you behind when I take off from here. I suppose I've been a little too much on my guard and I do apologise if I've hurt your feelings in some way. Now are we on speaking terms again?'

'Of course,' she said, drawing a little away from him.

'Thank God for that. I'll admit I'm used to temperament, but I wouldn't have expected you to be exhibiting it so early.'

She asked without really knowing why, 'Was Berenice Esmond temperamental?'

'Very,' he said tightly, and deftly turned her towards him to kiss her. She submitted, but it required an effort. On the ship, she had accepted caresses like this so casually, but now they irritated her. And for some reason she felt ashamed of herself.

When he let her go Warren said, 'Now fetch your hat and we'll play a love scene down by the creek. We've got to have you ready for that test.'

Reya fetched her hat, and this time when she played the scene he demanded of her, she knew without a doubt that she had done a lot better. It was odd, if she'd wanted it, she could have become quite keen on the idea of becoming

127

an actress. She was even beginning to believe that she did have some potential. After all, Warren was a man of experience.

Back at the homestead, they ate the lunch Everlie had prepared for them, and then Warren asked Reya, 'What about coming out in the car and looking for the others?'

After a second, she declined. She just didn't want to look as though she were chasing after Jackson ... when he had gone, she wandered into the garden and tried to analyse what had happened to her lately. Only one thing emerged, and that was that she was quite obsessed by Jackson Brand. She was mad, she thought, to continue to stay here under the circumstances. Yet to go before E. came back seemed ridiculous. Once her aunt was home, she could be of real help to her during her convalescence. Surely it would happen soon. Tom, she was positive, wouldn't want to stay away any longer than was necessary, for although Jackson was keeping an eye on Coolabah Creek, he still had Big Sky to look after.

As for Warren, she knew that only as a last resort would she take the plunge and attempt this acting thing. Of course it was unfair of her not to be completely honest with Warren about it. She should tell him to forget about her—to go back to Sydney and find some other girl to play Marie. Yet it was not as easy as all that. Warren was very tenacious, even though she had never pretended to be anything but dubious about it all. She wondered vaguely if his fixation on her had anything to do with the fact that she did bear a slight physical resemblance to Berenice Esmond—a resemblance that Margaret Alford at least had noticed.

Reya had turned back towards the house with the intention of blowing the cobwebs from her mind with a horse ride, when she stopped dead in her tracks, her pulse beat quickening. Jackson's station wagon had just pulled up on the gravel. For a second she stood quite still and then she began to walk towards the homestead very quickly, feeling the pricking of stiff, dried out grasses on the sides of her sandalled feet. Jackson had left the car and the sun struck down on his dark curling hair as, with his back towards her, he made for the house. Then quite abruptly he turned and saw her and came back. Her heart did crazy things.

'Hello! I was looking for you, Reya. I'm driving over to Coolabah Creek and wondered if you and Warren would like to come.'

She was staring at him as if he was the angel Gabriel. Just to see him, to hear his slightly drawling voice calling her by her name—it made her want to live for ever.

'Warren's not around, but I'd love to come,' she said quickly.

He frowned and she thought, 'He doesn't want to take just me.' But she didn't care what he wanted. He had invited her, and she was going. She said, 'I'll get my sunglasses. Will you wait? Or are you coming inside?'

'I'll wait,' he said, with a level and very speculative look. 'Let Everlie know we're going, will you?'

He went back towards the car and Reya hurried to her room. She had a mad notion that Jackson might drive off without her as she changed out of her jeans and shirt and put on the red and white Love dress. She wondered where Marlene was, but all she really cared was that she wasn't here. She brushed on some subtle grey-green eyeshadow, then clipped a red band around her forehead to keep her hair in order. She was in a mad mood, in contrast to her mood of the morning. 'Warren deadens me,' she thought. '*He* revives me.' It was time to admit to herself openly that she'd never got over Jackson Brand—that he was more than half the reason why she had had to come back to Australia.

If she was in love with the outback, then Jackson was its personification. It tallied with the fact that she was as un-certain of his reception of her as she was of that of his land. Because while she knew he didn't want her here, she also knew that he felt at least a physical attraction towards her. He'd actually said she was sexy—and to be considered

129

sexy was *something*, she told her mirror image determinedly before she dashed off to let Everlie know where she—and Jackson—were going.

He was smoking when she reached the car, a few minutes later, and he leaned across and opened the door for her. His quizzical expression told her that he'd taken in the fact that she'd changed her dress for his benefit, and meeting his eyes she quickly veiled her own.

'Jeans can be hot,' she excused herself. 'This dress is—very cool.'

'Oh, don't apologise for your appearance,' he said dryly. 'I'm all admiration. Your legs are very easy on the eye, too. However, I won't be free to admire them for a while,' he added as he started up the car and drove off. 'Did you tell Everlie where we were going?'

'Yes.'

'What have you been doing with yourself today? I thought Warren had decided to spend the day with you.'

'We went down by the creek this morning, and did a love scene,' she said deliberately, and looked at him out of the corner of her eye to see how he reacted. His profile was strongly compelling and ultra-masculine despite—or even in a way because of—the thick black curling hair that fell across his forehead and at the back brushed the collar of his dark cotton shirt. He didn't react to her statement at all except that she saw a nerve move in his jawline.

'I presume you're talking about this film you're so keen to have a part in,' he said. 'I hope you played your scene convincingly.'

'I think so,' she said. 'Warren says I have a lot of potential. Arthur thought so too—he's the man who owns the flat at Pott's Point,' she concluded blandly. She shivered slightly as she said it, and this time Jackson reacted with a frown, then drew long and hard on his cigarette before he crushed it out in the ashtray on the dashboard.

'There are two distinct sides to Reya Barberton, aren't there?' he said then. 'Of one, I was completely unaware till

130

just recently—the girl with dramatic ambitions. I'd thought all you ever wanted was'—he glanced at her dress —'love.'

'Then you were wrong, weren't you?' she said flippantly. It gave her a feeling of safety that he wasn't harping on his favourite theme—the schoolgirl crush on him that she was always denying so angrily.

'Hmm,' he said. 'Well, I must admit it's better this way.'

One point to him, she thought with a mental shrug, and was thankful there was a gate open at that point.

It wasn't till later when they were driving across Coolabah Creek property that either of them had anything more to say, and then it was on a far less personal subject.

'They're the wethers in this paddock, aren't they?' Reya asked a little stiffly, making an effort to break a silence that was beginning to bother her.

'That's right,' Jackson agreed, and proceeded to expand on the subject, falling in with her attempt at being impersonal. 'We're fortunate in being able to keep our wethers here, as they produce the best wool—I presume you know that. Graziers on smaller properties or with less pasture available have to sell their wethers and keep their fodder for breeding ewes. I don't suppose you're familiar with our policy, but as a result of it our wool has a big reputation in the western districts.'

She murmured something and looked into the sunshine where the sheep were scattered widely over a paddock so immense she couldn't see a fence in any direction.

'We still specialise in medium-fine wool,' Jackson continued almost soothingly. 'Even though our cheques would be fatter if we concentrated on stronger wool. It's not guesswork, you know—a case of accepting whatever turns up. It's a matter of careful scientific breeding to produce exactly what we want. That's why we buy our rams from a merino stud and select our breeding ewes with a great deal of care . . . Interested?' he queried with a slightly sceptical smile. 'Or are you competely caught up with drama these days? Admittedly there's very little of *that* connected with wool growing.'

'I am interested,' she said warily, not sure whether or not he was baiting her—and subtly pointing out how alien to her sort of thinking his world was. 'But of course I don't know much about it—and don't pretend to. Uncle Tom never talked to me much about his work—I was only a schoolgirl then.'

'You should have come along with Warren the last couple of days,' he commented carelessly, and she almost answered, 'So I should have—but I was quite obviously not invited.'

He had slowed down in the shade of some trees near the deep waters of a tank that reflected the blue colour of the cloudless sky. 'It will soon be time to make a seasonal check of all the tanks and drains,' Jackson said. 'Silt has to be cleared out so we can make the most of any water we're lucky enough to get from summer thunderstorms.'

Reya nodded, frowning. This was one of her uncle's tanks, even if Jackson would persist in talking continually about what '*we*' do, and while it looked healthy enough now, she realised that maintenance work was essential. She said thoughtfully, 'Uncle Tom will have to come back soon, I expect. He can't leave the place for long at a crucial time like the start of the summer. Mack—well, Mack is nice, but I know he always has to be told, and *you* can't be expected to attend to his briefing all the time.'

Jackson stepped on the accelerator. 'Oh, your uncle has no worries. Besides, I've put Bill March in.'

Reya didn't ask him then what he meant, and she didn't find out fully till some time later.

Presently they stopped at the yards where Mack and Bill March were marking lambs and Jackson left the car to speak to them. When he came back he told Reya, 'Bill suggests we might like to come over to the homestead for dinner. Will that interfere with your plans? Do you need to get back to the Big Sky in a particular hurry?'

'No,' she said after a second. 'But what do you mean—

132

over to the homestead? To my uncle's homestead?'

'Sure. Linette will toss a few more potatoes in the baking dish. It will be all right.'

Reya was staring at him and she felt her skin begin to prickle. 'But do you mean these people are—are living in my aunt's house?'

'Where else would you expect them to live?' he asked with raised eyebrows. 'There's no room in Mack's cottage, and not another bungalow on the property. They're not disturbing your things,' he added after a moment, 'if that's what's bothering you. You may remember there are four bedrooms.'

Reya listened and her thoughts seemed to be flying about in all directions. She knew her uncle had said Jackson would keep an eye on things, but what a cheek, what a high-handed thing to do—to let other people move in, take over the house.

'Does my uncle know?' she asked, hostility plain in her voice.

'Of course your uncle knows. What are you so upset about? Do you think I should have told you too?—asked your permission?'

'No,' she said, her voice low. Yet all the same, in a way she did think he should have told her what was going on. But of course it was typical that he had not—it was part of his policy of excluding her ... So what sort of a fool was she, persuading herself that she—felt anything for him but antagonism? She sat back in her corner and said very little for the remainder of the drive.

It was an odd sensation to be welcomed at Coolabah Creek by someone other than her aunt. Linette March was in her late twenties, plump, blonde, quite pretty, and very much a country girl. She wore a sleeveless cotton dress, and she was perspiring a little. She welcomed Reya affably when Jackson introduced her, and added, 'Come on in. Dinner will be another forty minutes or so—Bill should be in by then. You know where everything is, Reya. Have a wash up if you feel like one—there's a couple of spare towels on the rail in the bathroom. I'll get some cool drinks. Beer?'

Her glance included both of them, and Jackson said, 'Beer sounds great to me, Linette. For you too, Reya?'

'No, thank you—just lemon squash or something please.'

Linette disappeared to the kitchen—to Aunt E.'s kitchen —and Reya looked around the sitting room with faint bewilderment. It looked just the same. There were flowers, and it was all nicely dusted and polished, just the way her aunt kept it. There had never been any photographs, but there was the usual scattering of magazines and farming journals. It struck her, rather oddly, that it looked like any woman's sitting room. Not just Aunt E.'s ... She sat down in one of the chairs and Jackson sat down too and stretched out his long legs comfortably.

After a moment she said accusingly out of her thoughts, 'Warren and I could come back here.'

He raised his eyebrows. 'Two women both trying to be mistress of the same house? No fear—that never works. Besides, while Linette likes visitors it wouldn't be fair to land her with house guests not of her own choosing.'

Reya looked at him angrily. Why should he be the one to make the decisions all the time? Why should he say who was to stay in her uncle's house and who was not to? *She* had more right to be there than Linette and Bill March.

Linette came in with the drinks then and ten minutes later Bill came home. Without caring whether Jackson thought she should or not, Reya went out to the kitchen with Linette. After all it was her aunt's kitchen. She said firmly, 'I'll help you with the dinner, Linette.' And Linette said equally firmly, 'No, thank you, Reya—I'd rather manage on my own. You go back to the menfolk.'

Reya bit hard on her lip and turned away. She wasn't going to join the men, though. She would take a walk in the garden and let her anger simmer down. As she reached the door, Linette said, 'Oh, by the way, my sister's coming over from Bourke tomorrow to stay for a few days. I was going to shift the things from one of the bedrooms. You'll be moving out the rest of your stuff tonight, I suppose, will you?'

For a second Reya was speechless. Then she said briefly, 'You'd better ask Jackson,' and went quickly away before she lost her head and said anything more.

She didn't enjoy her dinner that night, beautifully cooked and appetising though it was. She felt at odds with everyone, and she knew her eyes were smouldering. She refused to look at Jackson who was sitting opposite her, telling herself that she hated him, and yet knowing that she was being unreasonable. After all, someone had to run Coolabah Creek while Tom was away, and he had left Jackson in charge, apparently with no restrictions. 'Calm down,' she told herself, as she made a pretence at eating. Queen's pudding following the main course and she managed a little of it. Linette took the coffee into the sitting room and Reya didn't offer to help with the washing up, although she hadn't seen the housegirl about. Linette could have it all to herself, if that was the way she wanted it—and this was what she did, with complete cheerfulness. When she came back to join the others—the men had been talking sheep and Reya had been half listening, half seething—she said equably, 'I need another bedroom, Jackson, for my sister. Reya was wondering if she'd be able to take the rest of her things tonight.'

'Sure,' said Jackson. 'There's plenty of room in the car.' He glanced at his watch. 'Run along and get the rest of your stuff together now, will you, Reya? We must be off presently.'

Reya went without a word. But she didn't go into the bedroom she always thought of as hers. She went instead to Warren's room. He had left a suitcase, and there were a few shirts and underthings in the drawers, and some other clothing still hung in the wardrobe. She packed up everything carefully and taking the suitcase on to the verandah, left it by the steps before she went back to the sitting room.

Jackson stood up instantly. 'Ready?' She nodded. 'Then

we'll be on our way. Thanks for the dinner, Linette—you're a beaut cook. You're a lucky man, Bill,' he added with a smile. 'I'll be over again in a day or two and have a word with you about the hogget shearing. Goodnight.'

Reya managed to make her own farewells sound civil enough. She knew that she had been behaving badly and was aware that Linette had long ago given up trying to make conversation with her. Of course the situation was not Linette's fault, but all the same she could have been tactful enough to allow Reya *some* rights to the house that was to some extent her home. All Reya could hope—and she hoped it quite desperately—was that her aunt and uncle would soon be back.

'Is this the lot?' Jackson asked as he carried the single suitcase over to the car.

'Yes.' She stopped at that. She didn't think it necessary to explain to him that she had decided not to pack her own things, that she planned soon to be back here.

Neither of them spoke until they were well on their way, and then he asked her unexpectedly, 'What got into you tonight, by the way? I've never known you so uncommunicative. Linette's a nice young woman, yet if I'm not mistaken you decidedly gave her the cold shoulder. It doesn't speak well for your hopes of making the grade as an actress if you can't put on a better show than that. What got you offsides?'

'What do you think?' she said moodily. 'I don't like seeing other people taking over my aunt's home.'

'Good God!' he exclaimed. 'E. wouldn't mind. What would you suggest, anyhow? That the Marches should camp out under the stars? Bill's not there for ornamental reasons, you know—he's taking over the responsibility of the property. There's a lot of work to be done yet before any of us can consider taking a vacation.'

'So my uncle will be back soon,' she said argumentatively.

'I think not,' he retorted. 'I've suggested to him that he

should take his holiday now for your aunt's sake. In which case, he won't be back for a month.'

Reya drew a sharp breath. Jackson Brand certainly liked to throw his weight around! It was just typical of him to interfere and 'suggest' to Tom what he should do—and then go so far as to install his own overseer in Tom's house. Bitterly, she perceived part of the purpose behind it all—to oust her. It was totally incredible, yet she knew that it was so. She thought of the solitary suitcase in the back of the car and knew a momentary qualm. She wasn't winning this battle, that was clear. Without doubt, she was going to have to leave—and soon. That was, if Tom took up his 'suggestion'. And with a feeling of helplessness, she supposed that he would—especially as Jackson had cunningly said it was for E.'s sake.

She had been looking out at the darkness, the great silence and emptiness of the plains, but now she turned to Jackson resolutely and said, 'My uncle won't take his holiday now. Why should he take so much notice of what *you* think?'

'Why would you imagine? But if you're trying to attribute some obscure and foul motive to me, you couldn't be more wrong. I'm thinking solely of the Westwoods. E. doesn't have any close friends in Sydney. She needs Tom around and I've made it possible for him to stay with an easy conscience, and without being bugged by the thought of work undone or of placing too great a burden on me. I can spare Bill March. I've another man moving up and about ready to take on the job of overseer, and I've Milton Lane—for the time being, anyhow.'

'I, I, I,' thought Reya angrily, but something was worrying at her mind. Jackson Brand was busy moving everyone around like pieces on a chessboard—just as if he owned the whole show. And then he said something that shocked her to the core, for it made her realise that he *did* own the whole show.

'In the twelve or so years that Tom Westwood's been running Coolabah Creek for me I've been fully aware that I

137

couldn't have had a better manager. I'd be a poor sort of boss if I couldn't do something for him and his wife now. So I suggest you stop thinking solely of yourself and your stubborn determination to score over me, and snap out of it. Tom's not to come rushing back here just for your convenience. You've asked Livingston-Lowe along—he's obviously enamoured of you, and you've got the offer you wanted from him. When it pleases you, you'll disappear into the blue with him. Do us all a favour and make it soon, will you?'

Reya leaned back in the seat beside him, listening, feeling utterly appalled. So he owned Coolabah Creek—her uncle was just the manager. Several things began to slip into place. *That* was why Marlene had said what she did about the Westwoods coming under a different category—and about Reya's trying to impress Warren. And *that* was why E. had always listened so hard to Jackson's opinions and advice. Of course, everyone—even Jackson, even E. and Tom, she supposed—had taken it for granted that she knew. And she hadn't had a clue! Oh, what a fool she had been! Now she and Warren were—*bludging* on the boss's hospitality. She closed her eyes exhaustedly. No, quite decidedly Reya Barberton was not winning this battle. She had lost in many ways. The outback, with Jackson Brand's help, was quite decidedly rejecting her. She would have to be on her way—before it was too late to salvage anything.

She raised her lids and saw in the light of the dashboard Jackson's hand reach into the glove box for cigarettes.

'Smoke?'

'No, thank you.' Her voice was scarcely audible. He lit up and she didn't turn her head to look at him. She didn't have to, because she could see him with perfect clarity in her mind's eye. The dark curling hair, the straight nose, the square intelligent forehead—even the curve of his mouth, and those direct and startlingly blue eyes.

So what did she feel about him? Did she hate him? Or did she love him? It didn't really matter either way, because he didn't want her here. She would have to give in,

138

to tell Warren she was ready to go, and make, that way, a not completely ignominious exit. Perhaps this way she would eventually forget Jackson Brand.

It was odd that at that instant she recalled something he had said to her not so long ago: Take care who you fall in love with. She felt a sudden desperate sick upsurging within her. Her heart seemed to cry out to the man beside her, and she closed her eyes dizzily. She felt she would give anything on earth for him to stop the car now and take her into his arms and do anything he wanted with her. Even if it was just because he found her sexy . . .

'I must be mad,' she thought, because the car was slowing down and in a few seconds it had come to a standstill. She closed her eyes, she felt she couldn't breathe.

And then he said in a low voice, 'Did you hear that?'

Her lids flew up and her heart began to pound. 'What?'

'A dingo.'

The windows were open and now that the motor was switched off everything was dead still, dead silent. Reya listened, and presently she heard it. Somewhere over the empty plains—where she could discern vague shapes of sheep among the scattering of trees—a weird and spine-chilling howling, and at the same time, far out on the horizon she saw the flicker of eerie blue lightning.

'My God, I wish I had my rifle with me,' Jackson said tensely. He drew on his cigarette and reached forward to switch on the ignition again. Then he changed his mind and said, his voice low, 'Come here.'

The next few minutes were both heaven and hell. She was in his arms and he was kissing her—kisses such as she had never known, that seemed to draw the soul out of her. She was all warmth and desire, her body melted against the hardness of his, her fingers were in the curling hair at the back of his head. She didn't want it to stop—ever. Through the thin cotton of her dress—her Love dress—she could feel the warmth of his hand cupped against her breast . . . When he let her go and moved along the seat away from her she wanted to weep. She was filled with an excruciating mixture of agony and shame and desire.

He said nothing, though she longed for him to speak— to hear him say anything, to explain himself, to excuse himself, to ask her if she had minded. Anything at all.

Then the dingo howled again and he said, his voice uneven, rough, 'I'm going home for that rifle.'

In no time at all they were on their way, and Reya stared through eyes blurred with tears at the summer lightning playing far out on the flat horizon.

CHAPTER EIGHT

There were still lights on at the homestead when they reached Big Sky, although it was fairly late. Reya went straight to her room to comb her hair and to put a little colour on a face that was dead white. In the mirror, her eyes looked enormous and black and utterly lost. She couldn't bear the thought of Warren or the others seeing her like that, but she knew she must face them. They might put all sorts of interpretations on it if she didn't appear.

Well, Warren claimed she had potential as an actress, though Jackson hadn't admired her performance just now at Coolabah Creek, and staring at herself in the glass she couldn't think how she was going to hide the fact that she was stricken. Yet why should she be stricken? Nothing had happened, except that she had discovered that Jackson was her uncle's boss and that she wasn't going to be able to hang on like a leech to her precious outback. A month in Jackson's house would be impossible, and if she didn't go of her own free will, then she had no doubt he would 'suggest' she do so.

And the other—minor thing that had happened, she thought wearily, was that she and Jackson had had a—a necking session. She put it to herself like that, deliberately crudely, and hated herself for doing so. Anyhow, it was a fact that *nothing* earth-shaking had happened. She had a few mental adjustments to make, that was all. She would come through it. She lowered her lashes a little and managed a smile that looked, even to her own eyes, horribly secretive, and far from reassuring. Well, she couldn't help what anyone thought, they could prove nothing, for there was nothing to prove. Yet it was with the most stultifying inner reluctance that she finally went along to the sitting room.

Marlene and Milton had been playing chess, and tonight it was Warren who was turning the pages of a magazine. He looked up without smiling as Reya entered the room—annoyed with her, she thought in dismay, for going out with Jackson. He was not the only one who was annoyed either, as she realised when Marlene asked her icily, 'Where's Jackson?'

She decided on surprise tactics and said animatedly, 'There's a dingo out in the paddock. Jackson's getting his rifle to go after it.'

They all stared at her for a moment and then Jackson came through the doorway, his face dark and hard and expressionless.

'I'm going out after a dingo. Want to come along, Warren?'

'I don't think so,' said Warren briefly.

Jackson looked at the others—but didn't include Reya. 'Anyone else? Marlene? Milton?'

Yes, they would go, and in a matter of minutes, Reya and Warren were alone.

'You should have gone too,' said Reya, sinking down on the lounge, though she would far sooner have gone straight to bed.

He ignored that, and came to stand and look down at her. 'What made you run off with Jackson this afternoon?'

She raised her eyebrows. 'I didn't run off. Jackson invited us both, but you weren't around.'

He studied her face for a few seconds and then said thoughtfully, 'You like him a little too much, don't you? He's the reason for your apathy about *South of the Gulf*.'

'Don't be ridiculous,' she said instantly, but she felt the colour staining her cheeks and was thankful the lamp was on the other side of the room. 'We just went over to Coolabah Creek. There's a couple living in the homestead now. Bill March is running things while my uncle's away.' She paused, then hurried on, 'They're expecting a visitor from Bourke and wanted another bedroom, so I—I brought your clothes back. My uncle and aunt won't be back for a month.' She said it as though it hadn't been a shock to her, and she knew that it was perfectly true. Tom would do as Jackson—his *boss*—had 'suggested'.

Warren sat down beside her and took out cigarettes. She had never accepted a smoke from him, and now as he lit up and the familiar scent of cloves was wafted in her direction, she thought of how often they had stood together on the ship, the darkness of the ocean rolling by, his arm about her, and it all seemed to belong to a past so distant it was quite unreal.

'You know,' he said, blowing smoke, 'it's time we were leaving here. You *are* coming with me, aren't you?'

'Yes,' she said hesitantly, although she had already made up her mind about that. 'But I don't really know about taking up acting, Warren, or playing in *South of the Gulf*——'

He frowned. 'You're not going to back out of it, Reya, when you've more or less made me a promise in various ways. We'll give you a test in Sydney. You're very photogenic—I already know that—and you respond well to teaching. I'll be surprised if you don't come out of it extraordinarily well. I can get Jon to tailor that role to fit you exactly, and I predict that you'll be brilliant.' He looked at her hard. 'I'm not going to let you off. When I've made up my mind, I get what I want, and you're going to be another Berenice Esmond.'

Reya listened with a feeling of helplessness, rocked more than a little by Warren's vehemence, his refusal to let her make a choice. *Had* she made him any promises? Or was it going to happen the way he wanted it no matter what she said? When it came to alternatives—she knew she couldn't go back to the Alfords, and what else was there? As she went worriedly over it all in her mind, Warren reached out and drew her against his shoulder, and she didn't resist, not even when he kissed her, but the thought flashed through her mind, 'I shan't altogether be another Berry Esmond—I shall never be his mistress.' That was just a little bit funny, because Warren had never been intent on

143

making her that. Jackson Brand's attentions to her, in fact, had been far more pressing in that particular way than Warren's.

'Tomorrow?' Warren asked, his lips against her hair. 'Shall we get away tomorrow?'

'The day after,' she said with an effort. 'I still have things to collect from Coolabah Creek.'

'All right,' he agreed. 'We'll go to Coolabah Creek in the morning, and leave early the following day.'

They parted for the night soon after that. The others hadn't returned and Reya wondered if the dingo had been shot. Lying in bed, she thought uneasily about Warren and her own future and the speed with which everything seemed to be changing. In her own mind, she was certain that she would have parted from Warren in a very short time, and be heading back to Coolabah Creek just as soon as her aunt and uncle had returned. So what was the matter with her? Had she no pride? Moreover, wasn't it possible that by that time Marlene, who had settled in at Big Sky as if it were her home, would once more be engaged to Jackson Brand, and that this time she would marry him?

The very thought hurt, and her whole being cried out against it. She knew painfully and without doubt that despite everything, what she wanted more than anything in life was to be Jackson Brand's wife . . .

When she went out for breakfast in the morning, she discovered that other people had their problems too. Warren and Milton were already at the table, and so was Jackson, and Marlene, who had been talking to her father on the telephone, was just about to take her place. She said, as she sat down angrily, 'My father must be in his dotage! He's made up his mind positively—or my stepmother has made it up for him—to put in a manager, take a trip to Fiji, and retire to the coast. It's just *pathetic*! Trisha will spend his money like water, he'll drink too much from sheer boredom, and finish up dying of a heart attack. If he hadn't let that woman hoodwink him into marriage he'd have been perfectly happy to spend the rest of his life on

Lilli-Pilli and die with his boots on. However, there's nothing I can do about it. But it's occurred to me that Milton should put in for the managership. Would you recommend him, Jackson? And could we go over today, to get in on the ground floor, as it were?'

'As you please,' said Jackson not very agreeably. 'I'll give you a recommendation, Milton, if it's needed.'

'Thanks,' said Milton carelessly, and Reya thought he was rather dull not to have noticed Jackson's shortness. But perhaps he had, and didn't care. He would take the day off in his own interests regardless of leaving Jackson short-handed, with Bill March at Coolabah Creek.

The dingo, Reya learned presently, had not been shot, but it had murdered three lambs—which perhaps accounted largely for Jackson's bad humour. Reya found him moody and unapproachable, and her heart sank at the prospect of revealing to him her plans of leaving Big Sky the following day.

She didn't have an opportunity to talk to him privately until later, when Marlene and Milton had driven off and Warren was doing something with his camera. The minute she saw him stride through to the verandah, his hat in his hand, she followed him quickly. He was wearing a navy shirt today and narrow-legged dark drill trousers, and he looked like a thundercloud except for the blueness of his eyes.

'Well? What's the trouble now?' he asked unencouragingly as Reya stopped beside him.

She felt herself quake. It was impossible to believe that what had happened between them had ever happened—and yet, in fact, it was nothing.

She said determinedly, 'Warren and I are leaving tomorrow. It's been kind of you to allow us to stay here, but as my uncle won't be back for a while, we can't impose on your hospitality any longer. You've done your duty, and as you said, it wasn't *your* idea to have us here.'

He didn't deny what she had said. His dark brows rose

145

and then descended, and his eyes seemed to pierce her like hailstones.

'Where do you intend to stay in Sydney?'

She coloured deeply. 'I don't see that that concerns you. But don't worry, I'll ask my uncle to help me find somewhere. Anyhow, you've got what you wanted.'

He didn't ask what she meant by that. He said coldly, 'Let's hope you get what you really want, too. I certainly hope you intend seeing Tom. But above all, don't be rash—think hard before you let yourself in for anything—anything at all. It's not for me to question what you do, and personally'—he almost bit it out—'I'm *not* concerned. But in the absence of your aunt and uncle I'd be lacking in conscience if I didn't urge you to watch your morals, and not to act too liberated.'

'You aren't always so conscientious about my morals!' she flung at him. She drew a deep breath, remembering how he had held her in the darkness last night—how close they had been, *physically* close, because she hadn't a clue what had been going on in his mind. It was laughable to think *he* was preaching to her about morals, when he had hardly done his best to guard them.

'If you're referring to what happened—or didn't happen—last night,' he said levelly, 'I agree. Frankly, I'll be glad to see you go tomorrow . . . Was there anything else?'

She bit her lip hard before she was steady enough to answer. 'Warren and I will drive over to Coolabah Creek this morning to get the rest of my luggage. Then we can make an early start tomorrow.'

Jackson gave her a last coldly searching look. 'Please yourself,' he said briefly, and turned away.

Warren took her to Coolabah Creek later on in the morning and left her there to pack up while he drove out to the paddock where Bill March and Mack were mustering the fourteen-month-old hoggets ready for the shearers, who were coming in a few days' time. Linette had gone to Djilla to meet her sister, the housegirl said, and so Reya had the house virtually to herself. Nevertheless, she felt an intruder.

She was conscious now that the house wasn't really E.'s, and that while the Marches were here it belonged to them. When she had packed up, she left her suitcase on the verandah and wandered down to the creek, waving to Spence in the horse-yards as she went.

The sun was burningly hot and the air was very still, and, down under the coolabahs, she lay in the old hammock and swung slowly, staring up at the pale sky where an eagle drifted, almost motionless in the windless sky. It was going to be a hot summer, and this was the beginning of it. The water no longer sang in the creek, but the cicadas in the trees burst into a deafening drumming that made her head throb. It was all part of the remote, mysterious outback, and for her it had—and always would have—an almost irresistible fascination. Dreamily she wondered what it must have been like to be an explorer when the vast inland of the continent was mostly unknown— or to have been one of those sheep farmers in the early days, pushing out with their flocks into virgin country, looking for pastures to take up and grow the wool that was Australia's wealth. The peace—the timeless, listening quality of the land—it enthralled, and yet it could be deadly. The outback had killed many men it had enticed. Jackson had told her once that he was like the outback—tough and brutal and practically impossible to live with. And he too had enthralled her. For a moment Reya wished that she had never been sent here as a schoolgirl, had never felt the arms of this country reach out and seize her, as if they would either crush the life out of her or love her and hold her for ever.

Yes, the outback and Jackson Brand were very much alike ...

It was a relief when she heard Warren's car as he returned, and could slip out of the hammock and forget, as she walked up to the homestead, the troubling thoughts that had filled her mind.

Everlie had lunch ready for them when they reached Big Sky, and Reya scarcely glanced inside her room where Warren had carried her suitcase. Afterwards, they agreed to take a last ride around, and Reya wished as she made her way to the saddling yard where Warren waited for her that it was Blackberry Tart she would be riding.

On Big Sky too, the men were mustering the hoggets, but Jackson had driven the utility out to inspect some of the tanks. He drove up later while Warren, leaving Reya in the shade of some mulgas, was taking some film of the men who were on motorbikes and working the sheep with the help of their dogs. The kelpies were alert, intelligent animals, trained to within an inch of their lives, and Reya found it exciting to watch the skill with which they managed the sheep, and their instant response to the low, whistled instructions of the men. For sure they were the reason why a station the size of Big Sky was able to operate with so small a labour force.

Reya saw the utility arriving and knew it was Jackson, and her heart began to thud, but she refused to turn her head and look in his direction. If he wanted to take any notice of her he would, and if he didn't, she was ready to ignore him too. But she knew very well that if he didn't come and speak to her—if he drove away without a word —it would be very hard to bear.

However, he came straight towards the trees where she still sat her horse, and as he pulled up and left the utility, she slipped from the saddle and stood waiting for him.

'You got your things from Coolabah Creek?' he asked, his glance taking her in quickly—her figure trim in the little red shirt and tightly fitting black pants.

'Yes,' she said briefly, her eyes lingering on his.

'You've been back home, of course. You got your mail? Did your aunt tell you the news?'

The news? Her heart gave a little premonitory leap of fear. She had forgotten it was mail day and hadn't looked for letters in her room. 'I didn't get my letters. What— what's the news?'

His blue eyes were expressionless. 'Tom's written me a formal acceptance of an offer I made him recently—to take over the managership of a fat lamb raising property I own in the Southern Highlands. As from January next year. That means that the Westwoods have finished with Coolabah Creek, and Bill March will stay on.'

Reya didn't quite take it in at first. Her mind went quite blank except for a voice repeating over and over in her head, 'The Westwoods have finished with Coolabah Creek.' She stood staring at Jackson Brand and slowly she began to make sense of what he had said. He had offered Tom another property, and Tom had accepted. Because, she thought, he would have had no alternative. And it was all part of Jackson's determination to get rid, once and for all, of Reya Barberton. It was—it was despicable, and it made her sick—sick. So sick she felt she was choking. There would be no coming back now—not ever. Today was the last day she would ever spend here. Tonight would be her last night. However much she wanted it, she would never see Jackson Brand again. It was no use hoping, dreaming, scheming, as she had last night. She had lost. A girl like her could never win a trick in a game with a man as hard and ruthless as Jackson Brand. Even her uncle didn't matter to him so long as he could do things his way.

She searched his face for signs of victory, and in the slight upward curve of his mouth—that mouth that had given such madly frustrating bliss to hers—she thought she found what she was looking for. But in the blue eyes that looked and looked at her, she could read nothing.

Nor could she find anything to say. Her mouth was dry and something seemed to have happened to the sun. The crystal clarity of the afternoon light had gone.

Jackson said, 'Your aunt will be pretty happy about it. She's had twelve years of loneliness and hardship.'

Reya half closed her eyes. The red of her own shirt was dazzling her. She remembered the native girl in the cloak of red parrot feathers, waiting in vain for her warrior lover to come back to her. That girl had been turned into a flower —Sturt's lovely Desert Pea—and Reya thought dimly, 'I wish I could be turned into a flower, and stay here for ever.' She looked up at Jackson again, at that hard, darkly tanned face and those astonishingly blue eyes, and she said stumblingly, 'You never wanted me here, did you?'

'You? What have you got to do with it? Haven't you got your new career?' he said.

They stared at each other, motionless, silent, for several seconds, and with complete illogic she felt she would have given her life for him to take her in his arms one last time —crush her, kiss her—she didn't care who saw them . . .

Then he said, coolly, 'We're going to have a storm shortly. You and Warren had better make for home right away. I'll see you tonight.' He turned quickly and went back to the utility, and Reya stood where she was and watched him drive over to where Warren was still watching the muster. Her feet felt leaden, her heart was dead.

Behind her, her horse moved restlessly and further along beneath the mulgas, Warren's mount whinnied nervously. Glancing up at the sky, Reya saw it had paled to almost white, and far out on the horizon clouds were swarming rapidly. The air, that had been very still, became a flurrying wind and the leaves of the mulgas made an urgent whispering sound.

Warren came hurrying towards her.

'There's going to be a storm. Let's get going. We should race it back to the homestead if we start right away.' He helped her into the saddle, mounted his own horse, and in minutes they were on their way, the horses moving side by side.

It was unnerving to see the pace at which the clouds were tumbling into the sky from the horizon. Lightning flashed like mirrors, illuminating them again and again, though as yet no thunder was to be heard. Warren was having a little difficulty controlling his mount, a more nervous creature than Reya's. The long stiff grasses bent as the wind raced up, bringing with it great dried out roly-poly bushes that bowled across the ground to fetch up against a clump of salt bush or the wires of a fence.

They rode from weird white sunlight into heavy cloud

150

shadow as the sky darkened, and when the first chords of thunder roared threateningly from the heavens, Warren's horse bolted. Reya's horse wasn't far behind, and they both went racing across the paddock like mad things. The crunch came when an enormous roly-poly crossed their path. Reya had her horse under control by then, but Warren's horse went mad, rearing up, snorting and whinneying, then careering off at a tangent. With a sense of shock, Reya saw it stumble and fall, with Warren underneath. The next instant the terrified creature had staggered to its feet and Warren was being dragged along the ground, one foot still in the stirrup, his camera and equipment scattered about.

'Free your foot!' Reya shouted as she spurred her horse to race after the runaway. It was terrible to see Warren's body bumping along the ground as the horse charged on. He had been dragged perhaps twenty yards when he finally freed himself, and by that time the rain had started—great heavy drops that came down drenchingly, blindingly.

Reya didn't know what to expect when she reined in and slid down from the saddle to where Warren lay on the grass. To her relief, he was most decidedly alive, and swearing heartily. He struggled to a sitting position as, holding on to her horse's reins, she leaned down and asked him anxiously, 'Are you badly hurt, Warren?'

His face looked grey as he tried to rise, and he swore again.

'My damned ankle—it's broken. Or it could be my leg. For God's sake get someone quickly—get a car—get a doctor. And get me out of this confounded rain!'

She looked around her helplessly. The nearest shelter was under some trees that were at least a hundred yards away, and she didn't see how she could possibly get him there. At least he hadn't broken his neck or cracked his skull, she thought. At least he was fit enough to be angry and demanding . . . She said, 'I'm sorry, but I can't get you out of the rain, Warren. You'll have to stay there while I go for help—I'll find Jackson. He has the utility. He might even be on his way back now.'

'Then for God's sake get a move on and don't stand there yapping!' Warren snapped, and she flinched. 'I wish to heaven I'd never come to this filthy godforsaken place in the first instance. I need a doctor, and Jackson Brand had better get me one quickly. I don't want to become a cripple at this stage of my life.'

'I'm sorry——' Reya began, but he glared at her and snarled out, 'Get moving, for Chrissake!'

She looked away from him, a frown creasing her brow. Disconcertingly, she was far from sure in which direction she should go. During that mad gallop they had got right off course, and now the rain had begun to fall so heavily it was almost blinding. But it was certain she couldn't leave Warren here indefinitely, and after an instant she climbed back into the saddle and pulling firmly on the reins, turned her horse's head. She had nothing but instinct to guide her, and on that she must rely. Her clothes were clinging to her, water dripped from her hair and if ever anyone looked, and felt, like a drowned rat, it was certainly Reya Barberton. It was terrible to have to leave Warren helpless on the ground, but there was nothing else to do. She only hoped she would find Jackson and not get herself lost in this obliterating rain . . .

The gods—or perhaps it was the presiding spirit of the outback—must have been with her, for she did find Jackson, and it was a triumph of a very private and personal kind, though a sad one, that on this, her last day, the outback should be kind to her. For instead of deluding her or leading her on with false promises, it led her straight to the man she sought.

Jackson was just about to climb into the utility while his men roared off on their motorbikes, the dogs in their boxes behind them. The rain had eased off a little, but lightning still split the sky and there was an almighty clap of thunder just as Reya reined in. For a ghastly second she thought her horse was going to bolt, but Jackson, rain dripping from the wide brim of his hat, stepped over quickly and took control of the horse.

152

'What's the trouble? What's brought you back here?' he rapped out, his blue eyes searching her keenly.

'Warren's had an accident. It's not serious, but he's hurt his ankle, he can't walk—and his horse has got away. Please—please will you come?'

'Of course.' He turned his head and let out the most piercing whistle she had ever heard, and immediately one of the bikes, now some distance away, turned and came racing back. Jackson helped her out of the saddle and installed her in the utility and then, when the motorbike skidded to a stop, he issued instructions—presumably about the horse and she didn't know what else—to the rider. Only seconds later they were driving across the paddock through rain that was still heavy though not blindingly so. It was only then that it occurred to Reya that in all probability she and Warren would not now be able to leave in the morning.

'What happened?' Jackson asked her presently.

'The horses bolted,' she explained, including herself in the accident. 'All those roly-polys—and then the thunder was bad. Warren's horse stumbled and fell and he was dragged some way.' She pushed back the dripping hair from her eyes. Her shirt was clinging to her like a second skin and she felt most uncomfortable in her soaking jeans, but there was nothing for it but to put up with it all, and for certain the man beside her was hardly bone dry!

He said thoughtfully, 'It's only a summer storm, it shouldn't interfere with the hogget shearing. We need storms like this to help us through the summer.' He gave her a quick sideways glance and a lopsided smile. 'I'm afraid I'm being callous. I've got a lot on my mind . . . Now exactly where is Warren?'

Reya was a little surprised to find she could give him fairly explicit directions, that she could remember where it was that they had left the track, but she could, and in not very long at all they had reached Warren, whose temper by this time, understandably, was rather more than frayed.

'You've taken long enough,' he complained as they left

153

the utility. 'I shall probably get pneumonia out of this as well as everything else.'

Jackson made no comment, but squatted down beside him, and with gently probing fingers, felt the ankle through the soft leather of the boot. The rain stopped abruptly and a brilliant shaft of sunlight struck through a gap in the clouds. Amazingly, there seemed to be no puddles on the ground—all that rain had soaked into the hungry red earth.

Warren said touchily, 'Don't bother messing around with my ankle, I'd rather have a doctor look at it. You may know a lot about sheep, but you know damn all about broken bones.'

'That's where you're wrong,' said Jackson, calm and unruffled. 'I've mended more broken limbs than you'd believe —and they didn't all belong to sheep. This boot of yours—it looks like it will have to be cut off. I'll see to that when we get back to the homestead . . . Now look, we're going to get you into the utility. Just keep your foot off the ground and lean on me all you like.'

Warren groaned and grimaced as Jackson got him to his feet, and Reya offered her shoulder too and he leaned on it unmercifully, and presently they were all installed, somewhat uncomfortably, in the front of the utility and driving back to Big Sky. Warren's face looked grey, and Reya asked sympathetically, 'Are you in pain, Warren?'

'Hellish pain,' said Warren.

'Probably the swelling,' said Jackson unfeelingly. 'It's a pity you hadn't thought to get your boot off right away— though you might still have done more harm than good if you'd been careless.'

'I'm sorry, Warren,' Reya said apologetically. She thought Jackson was rather unnecessarily callous. 'I should have known what to do to help you.'

'Now don't try to take all the blame,' said Jackson with a wry smile. 'If you should have known, then so should Warren.'

Conversation lapsed, and at long last they reached the

154

homestead, and together Reya and Jackson helped Warren inside to his room. There he lay on his bed and Jackson said sharply, 'Run along and get into some dry clothes, Reya. I've got to get Warren out of his wet gear now.'

She hurried to do as she was told, and when she returned, Warren was in pyjamas half lying on top of the bed, rubbing his hair dry with a towel, and looking anything but happy. Reya had seen Everlie and told her briefly what had happened, and she now came to ask if there was anything she could do, but Jackson appeared to have everything well in hand. He had a first aid kit handy as well as a pair of very businesslike scissors, and he had taken these up when Warren flung his towel aside and glared at him, his face white with pain—or was it fear?

'Get that woman to call a doctor before you do anything. It's done my ankle enough damage to be bucketed along that filthy track without having amateur attention now. Isn't there supposed to be a flying doctor available when these things happen?'

'You've got a swollen ankle,' said Jackson after a second. 'The flying doctor could be needed for a real emergency. I promise I know what I'm doing.'

'I doubt it,' said Warren angrily. 'Do you know I was dragged along the ground by one foot for a quarter of a mile? I want professional care, and I want the best. If I can't have the flying doctor, get someone out from Djilla.'

'You'd have a long wait,' said Jackson quietly. 'And that boot has to come off or you'll really be in pain.' He then proceeded firmly to cut away the boot and Warren was forced to submit.

Reya watched, and certainly Jackson managed skilfully and speedily, and then went ahead to examine the very swollen ankle, his fingers gentle and efficient-looking.

'I reckon you've got away with one small broken bone,' he pronounced finally. 'It won't take all that long to mend. I'm going to get it back into position and strap it, and to-morrow we'll get you in to Djilla.' Warren opened his mouth probably to protest, and Jackson said brusquely,

155

'Now shut up and submit to outback conditions. I'll do what I can to help you and afterwards you can have a stiff whisky. If you want the truth, the road to Djilla is impassable in long stretches after a storm like we've just had, so you'll have to accept my ministrations and make the best of it—and pray we don't have any more rain in the night.' He turned to Reya, who was standing uncertainly, sympathising with Warren's obvious pain, yet in no doubt at all as to Jackson's capability. 'You won't want to watch this. You can run along and pour a good stiff whisky for your friend ... Make it two,' he added as she turned obediently, feeling slightly nauseated now at the thought of Warren's pain.

She went quickly, and poured two whiskies with a hand that shook and set the glasses on a small tray. Then she looked out into the darkening garden and tried not to think of Warren and what was happening in his room.

A long time seemed to pass and then——

'You can breathe again,' said Jackson's slightly amused voice from close behind her. 'Let's have a look at you.' She hadn't switched on the lamp and he took her by the shoulders and turned her towards him. His hands remained where they were while he looked down at her. It was so nearly dark she was sure he couldn't see her pallor, but she knew that her body was trembling and that he must be aware of it through his contact with her shoulders.

'I thought it was only the sight of blood that upset you,' he said. 'Don't feel upset about Warren, I didn't hurt him much. And by the way, what I said about the road was true, in case you were wondering. It should be okay by morning if we have no more rain. You really lured him into the wilderness, didn't you? I'll bet that in Queensland he'll have first aid so close that if it's needed he won't even have to move a muscle to get to it ... now drink this down like a good girl and forget your agony.' One hand moved away to pick up a whisky glass. He held it to her lips and Reya raised a hand to steady it, her fingers touching his. She drank down the whisky and discovered his fingers had

156

closed gently round her wrist. It was like a bracelet of electricity that tingled up her arm and seemed to reach into her heart. Then he let her go, took up the other glass and swallowed down the contents.

'Mustn't forget the patient, must we?' he asked tautly, as he poured out another dose.

Shakily, Reya went ahead of him to see how Warren was faring.

CHAPTER NINE

MARLENE and Milton—possibly because of the storm—
hadn't returned from Lilli-Pilli and Jackson and Reya dined
alone. Neither of them had much to say. He seemed pre-
occupied, and she felt herself a mass of nerves, wondering
about tomorrow, wondering whether Jackson would take
Warren to Djilla for an X-ray and if so, what would happen
then. She half wished that none of this had happened, and
that early in the morning she and Warren could have been
on their way to Sydney, as they had planned. Not that she
was at all certain as to what she would do once she reached
Sydney. She would certainly contact Tom, but after that—
her mind was now a blank. However, it appeared that she
could put off any decisions about her future and would
have to wait and see what happened. She was in the hands
of fate—a mere pawn.

It was curious that at exactly that stage in her reflec-
tions Jackson said out of a long silence, 'Do you feel like
a game of chess tonight?'

Her nerves jumped as she raised her eyes and met his
quizzical blue gaze.

'Not—really,' she said jerkily, adding, 'There's not much
point in bothering to improve my chess now.'

'No.' He reached for the coffee pot that one of the housegirls had brought in quietly a few minutes ago. 'Still,' he
continued, his eyes compelling hers, 'it might keep us out
of mischief.'

'What do you mean?' she asked unwisely.

'What do you think I mean?' he drawled. 'We're virtually alone in the house with Marlene and Milton away.'
Despite the drawl, there was something tense in his voice
that ran like a saw edge along her nerves, and Reya felt
herself blush slowly crimson. He passed her over a cup of

black coffee and she thought he was looking amused—at her transparency, of course.

'Everlie and Don are in the house,' she said stiffly.

'In their own quarters,' he reminded her sardonically. 'And I'm the boss.'

She didn't answer, but drank her coffee quickly—it was scalding hot and brought tears to her eyes—then pushed back her chair.

'I'll go and see if Warren's comfortable. His ankle was painful——'

'He's very comfortable. I've given him something that will make him sleep until morning. *He* won't bother us tonight, either.'

She looked at him uneasily, but of course he hadn't meant anything other than that he had assured Warren of a restful night.

'Having your ankle pulled about first by a horse and then by a sheep farmer can be a painful business,' Jackson remarked. 'I don't think Warren was particularly grateful to me, but I'm fairly certain I've done a good job. However, an X-ray will confirm that tomorrow at the hospital. Do you think you're capable of driving in to Djilla? I'd come myself, but I'm busy at the moment and if Milton doesn't come back from Lilli-Pilli I shall be short-handed.'

'I shall be able to manage,' she said huskily.

'You may have to stay the night at the hotel if they decide to keep him in hospital for a day or two.'

She nodded. 'And then?' she wanted to ask, but didn't dare. She thought wretchedly, 'I wish we could go—that all this prevarication was over—that it was all finished with.'

Despite his reassurance, she left the dining room and went to look in on Warren. Sure enough, he was sleeping soundly. She stood there for a second. Jackson had followed her and she was deeply aware of him standing behind her, and somehow afraid to turn, to move in his direction.

All the same, she was taken by surprise when he suddenly caught her hard against him, with her back pressed to his body, and his hands cupped over her breasts. She seized his wrists and tried ineffectively to pull his hands away. Her heart was thudding against her ribs, and she panted out, 'Let me go! I wish—I wish this accident hadn't happened. I've—I've had enough of you and the outback! I want to go——'

She felt him tense and stiffen, but he didn't let go of her at once. His hands slid down to grasp her waist, and he said against her hair, 'Sometimes I've wished I might have just one hour alone with you before you go, Reya Barberton. Both of us might learn a great deal about each other that way. But it's probably best we should keep our distance.'

'Then keep it,' she breathed out. '*Keep* it. I know all I want about you. All I wish is you'd learn I'm not—not just a female body to be touched and—— An hour alone with you is the last thing I'd ask—two minutes generally prove to be too much.' He let her go and she stood there trembling, but managed to get out as he moved away, 'You're not the only one who will be glad when I leave this —this *one man's* land!'

When he had gone she stayed where she was, fists clenched, heart pounding, very much aware that what Jackson had said earlier was true. They were virtually alone in the house. She thought of what he had said about having an hour alone with her, and she knew with a kind of dreadful desperation that now, tonight, was probably the last time there would ever be any likelihood of its happening. So of course she must go at once, and lock herself in her bedroom . . .

Yet despite what she had said, some perverse part of her was unbearably tempted. She *longed* to be alone with Jackson—to learn whatever there was to learn. If she had to go —if she had to face up to the fact that soon she would never see him again—then she couldn't be hurt any more deeply.

After no more than two minutes, she had given in to her desires and gone like a sleepwalker through the house in search of him.

She found him on the verandah, leaning on the rail and

looking into the darkness. Faint light from a reading lamp in the sitting room fell across the floor behind him, and he turned towards her at the soft sound of her footsteps.

'What's the trouble?' His voice was flat, expressionless. 'I thought you'd taken yourself off to bed to get away from me.'

'No,' she said, and stopped where she was. She felt distinctly dashed, put in her place, by his indifference. He'd have been better pleased, quite plainly, if she *had* gone to bed and not bothered him again. She wondered if he was watching out for Marlene—hoping that she would be back tonight. Reya had no doubt at all that Marlene *would* come back to Big Sky—whether it was tonight or tomorrow made no difference, back she would come. To Jackson Brand.

'Why can't I hate him—or at least forget him?' she asked herself dementedly. Any other girl would do just that—any self-respecting girl. Because he had quite deliberately banished her aunt and uncle from Coolabah Creek so as to get rid of *her*. Yet here she was, seeking him out on the dark verandah simply because she couldn't keep away from him. It looked as though he could do or say anything at all to her, and she would still come crawling back, asking for more. She was, in fact, a hopeless case.

Meanwhile he was looking at her in the half dark, waiting for her to say what she wanted. She could see the quizzical inquiring upward tilt of his dark eyebrows. Obviously he wasn't going to help her out, and she said lamely, 'Earlier, you said we might have a game of chess. I thought——' Her voice trailed off and she moved uneasily to the rail some distance from him.

Jackson said nothing for a moment and from far off over the plains she heard a dingo howl and saw his faint frown. Then he said dryly, 'I've changed my mind about that. There's no point in our playing chess together. Or any other game.'

She turned her head and looked at him fully, and he looked back at her. He felt in his pocket for cigarettes, his

161

eyes still locked with hers, and then casually he took a couple of steps in her direction.

'Want one?'

Reya shook her head. The mad answer came into her head, 'My aunt wouldn't approve,' and she hovered on the edge of hysterical laughter. This open verandah with its green tiles, its wide roof, its restful cane furniture—this was the setting of her first deeply disturbing personal encounter with him. And that had been something she could never get out of her system—never. It had left a deep and ineradicable mark on her. It was like something begun and unfinished and forever crying out for completion ... With a mental effort, she tore her thoughts away from the path they were taking, because she knew too well where that led. She watched Jackson light up his cigarette and shake out the match, and then he put out a hand to her.

'Come along, then. We'll take a brisk walk around the garden. We can't stand here looking at each other for ever.'

Unwilling yet willing, she put her hand in his. But they never got as far as the garden because, without knowing how it had happened, she felt herself pulled into his arms, held closely, closely against his body, his arms enfolding her, his head bent, his lips finding hers. They stood locked in a long, long kiss that drained all the breath from her body, and then with a groan he released her.

He moved away and stamped out the cigarette he had let fall on the green-tiled floor.

Breathing shallowly and with difficulty, Reya watched him. Her body was in a turmoil. She felt an insensible despair that he had let her go like that. It was as if she had been dropped from a height and was falling, falling, through the air. Already her body anticipated the crushing pain it would feel when she hit the earth ... If he would only take her in his arms again—catch her—she would be saved. She said haltingly, as if out of a dream, 'Why—why did you let me go?'

'Why do you think?' His voice was low, savage, tense. 'Because I want to make love to you, that's why.'

Half a minute passed.

'I would—let you,' she said unsteadily. Her heart was beating hard, and she looked into his eyes that glinted dark and unreadable in the faint light.

He didn't move. He said, 'I know you would. And that's it, isn't it? There's this—thing between us. But it's *all* there is, do you hear? Absolutely all. It's just a damned physical thing, without rhyme or reason—one of nature's cruel tricks. Oh, I could make love to you, and you'd let me. You'd have let me when you were sixteen years old and I threw you down on that very couch over there.' He gestured with his dark head. 'Yes, it was all there for me to take even then, however much you've tried to deny it since. And we both know it. But if it happened it would be a prelude to nothing—so it won't happen.' He paused and she could hear him breathing hard. 'Despite my many faults, I do have a conscience, particularly where you're concerned. I wish to God that accident hadn't happened to complicate things. There's nothing that would set my mind more at ease than to know you were going to drive away from Big Sky tomorrow and get on with your theatrical career and never come back. Do you understand?'

Reya swallowed on the sob that had risen in her throat. 'No,' she said, and the sob showed. 'No, I—I don't understand. I can't. Why, when we—when we——' She stopped, unable to say any more.

Jackson moved away from her and sat down at one end of the cane lounger and lit another cigarette. She moved too and sat two feet away from him and said shakily, 'I would—I would like a cigarette, please.'

Almost absently he handed her the one he had already lit, and took another for himself.

'All the same,' he said flatly, 'think hard before you get yourself tied up with Livingston-Lowe.'

'I thought you considered him my type,' she said tiredly.

'He doesn't think enough of you. There are too many selfish, artificial people in his kind of world. If it weren't

163

for your ambitions, I'd advise you to forget him and go down south to stay with your aunt——'

'Don't advise me what to do,' she said fiercely. The cigarette had steadied her down a little, the torment in her body at least was subsiding. 'I'll make up my own mind. I'll probably be back in England soon,' she finished wildly.

'With Livingston-Lowe?'

'Does it matter? I have—plans.' Her voice broke a little.

'When did you make them?'

'When you told me what you'd done to my uncle.'

He stared at her. 'For God's sake, what did I do to your uncle? I offered him Clover Hills. He'll enjoy the challenge of switching from wool to fat lambs. He's an intelligent man—I have great confidence in him.'

'I don't mean that. What came before it—putting him off Coolabah Creek——'

He regarded her narrowly. 'Didn't you have a letter from Elaine?'

Reya started guiltily. There were letters in her room, half hidden under her hand mirror, which she hadn't picked up. She hadn't had time for letters today, and to tell the truth she had forgotten all about them—her mind had been so taken up, she reminded herself cynically, with more pressing matters.

'Didn't she tell you that Tom had decided not to come back?' Jackson pursued. 'He felt he'd subjected her to the outback for long enough.'

Reya didn't believe it. E. loved the outback—just as much as Tom loved it. She was sure of it. She was just about to tell him she didn't believe a word of what he was saying when car lights swept the drive, and in a few minutes, Marlene and the jackeroo climbed the steps to the verandah. Reya wondered in a panic if her hair was mussed, if her looks would give away what had just been happening between her and Jackson. Exactly what had happened? she asked herself cynically—except that he had kissed the breath out of her and she had practically asked him to make love to her. The memory washed over her in a

164

shaming wave, and she leaned back against the cushions of the lounge exhaustedly.

Jackson rose lazily to his feet, switched on the bracket lamp on the wall a little way along, and went to greet the newcomers. Marlene's eyes were bright and curious as she came straight along the verandah and sat down where she could get a full view of Reya. And she certainly made it a full view. She looked her over from her hair to her sandals —one of which had slipped off and lay on the floor. The two men after standing talking by the steps had gone inside—to fetch cold beer, Reya soon discovered. She managed by a hair's breadth to put a question to Marlene before one was asked of her, and her voice was only a little unsteady.

'How did Milton make out at Lilli-Pilli? Will your father give him the managership?'

Marlene shrugged. 'I don't see it's of any great interest to you. But if it will satisfy your curiosity, my stepmother has a candidate of her own—some crummy cousin whose people have a place that's probably about the size of a chicken run out Walgett way. If my father doesn't watch it, Lilli-Pilli's going to pass right out of the hands of our family. As things are at the moment, Trisha's the one who's giving the orders.' She flung herself back in the chair and crossed her legs. 'What were you doing sitting here in the dark with Jackson? Where's Warren?'

Reya flushed and then paled, and said nervily, 'Warren had an accident. His horse bolted in the storm and threw him. He's broken a bone in his ankle. Jackson—Jackson set it for him and tonight he had to give him something because of the pain. He's—he's asleep now.'

Marlene frowned and looked at her suspiciously. 'That's too bad. I thought you two would be pushing off any day now. I hope we're not going to have an invalid in the house for the next week.'

'It's not *your* house,' Reya retorted, unable to hold the words back.

'Not yet,' Marlene snapped back. 'But make no mistake,

it soon will be. So if you imagine you have a choice between Jackson and Warren, you're really fooling yourself. This is the last time you'll ever visit Big Sky, I assure you, now your uncle's left Coolabah Creek.'

At that strategic moment the men came to join them with a tray of glasses and a few cans of beer. Reya stood up quickly, her cheeks flushed. She told Jackson, her eyes bright, 'Not for me, thank you. I'm ready for bed.'

'I'll see you in the morning, then,' he said casually. 'I'll get on to the hospital first thing. You should be right for Djilla so long as we don't have another storm overnight. How was it coming over from Lilli-Pilli?' he asked Milton, turning away from her. Reya waited only to hear Milton say that it hadn't been too bad, and then with a murmured goodnight, she left them.

In her room, she stood quite still for a moment to compose herself and to think unwillingly about what Marlene had said about Jackson and Big Sky. Then she picked up her letters—there were two of them—from the dressing table, and flung herself exhaustedly on the bed to read them. One was from her aunt and the other was from Margaret Alford, and she opened her aunt's first and braced herself to discover how much truth or otherwise there was in what Jackson had said about Tom deciding he'd had enough of the outback.

She read through the letter quickly, and so far as she could see there was nothing to convince her either way, though the basics of the news were there, reported after E. had said she was making a wonderful recovery. 'We shan't be going back to Coolabah Creek. I'm just a little bit sentimentally sorry about that, mostly because of friends out there. However, Tom has agreed to take on Clover Hills—Jackson will have told you about it. He's been down to see the place already, and I'm sure we shall be very happy there. Unless you're doing something more exciting, darling—such as getting married, and I do like Warren—I'll be delighted if you'll come and stay with us. I'd have commandeered you long ago—you know that—but

Jackson wisely brought me to my senses. Now you've had experience of the world so much wider, as well as the opportunity to meet Warren. I didn't realise what an almost famous person he is till I read a paragraph in the news this morning about one of the stars in a TV series he made.

'This girl, Berenice Esmond, is in Melbourne just now, and one of the nurses said she was interviewed on TV and that she is *lovely*, and is due in Sydney in a few days. Perhaps you'll meet her—how I envy you such an exciting life! I wonder if she's to star in the film Warren is making in Queensland?'

Reya stopped reading to wonder too—and also to wonder if Warren had heard the news and if it would make any difference to his determination that *she* should play Marie. She had an intuitive feeling that if Berry Esmond turned up and wanted to come back to Warren, then Reya Barberton would quite simply be forgotten. Not that she would really care . . .

She finished the letter quickly, including the postscript that said, 'Tom will go back to Coolabah Creek later on to sort out our belongings and arrange for them to be sent to Clover Hills. No need for you to worry, Jackson will see that everything proceeds according to plan.'

Wonderful, wonderful Jackson, Reya thought, but there was an ache in her heart.

The other letter, from Margaret Alford, was simply an appeal to Reya to come back. There was a job waiting for her the minute she liked to take it, and as well, the tempting offer of a very substantial pay rise, and extra time off.

Reya simply couldn't work up an interest. Just at this moment there was only one thing she wanted, and she was fairly sick for it. Even though she knew she couldn't have it, it still prevented her from giving her mind to anything else or from being the least little bit realistic.

She had troubled dreams that night and waking very early in the morning lay listening to the laughter of kookaburras and the warbling of magpies, extra gay and lively after the rain. Soon she left her bed to shower and dress and see how Warren had fared during the night. Jackson was there before her; he had already inspected Warren's ankle and when Reya came in was lounging against the verandah doorway.

'Good morning,' he greeted her, his blue eyes flicking over her briefly. She thought faintingly that it was incredible that certain things could happen between a man and a woman and then they could meet the following day and be as cool and distant as strangers. She should, of course, thank God for it, and in a way she did, yet perversely she wished that Jackson wouldn't act so remotely. It struck a bitter blow at her heart that he could greet her so impersonally, and even while she was smiling at Warren—who appeared quite as irritable this morning as he had last night—she was thinking bleakly, 'Yes, you are like your country—inhospitable and uncaring despite its attractive appearance. There's nothing here for you, Reya Barberton—no water, no shade, no food or kindness or open arms. You're on your own.' Complete, uncaring rejection. 'You can die upon my bosom and I shall not care, your bones may lie unnoticed on my bleached grasses and my bland impersonal smile will reach out to the sky over the nothingness that was you.' *He* was like that, this man Jackson Brand. She would go and he would forget her, but for her it would be anguish, remembering . . .

'I've rung the hospital,' he said. 'I'm pretty sure I've done a good job on that bone, but of course we must have it X-rayed. How do you think you'll manage about driving to Djilla, Reya?'

Her heart seemed to stop. Without being conscious of it, she had hoped, since Milton was back, that he would come with them. But, as she had just reminded herself, he was hard. And she was on her own.

'If it doesn't appeal to you,' he said when she didn't answer, 'I'll ask Marlene to go along.'

'No, thank you,' she said coldly. 'I can manage.'

'Good.' He looked across at Warren. 'I don't think you need be over-anxious. I've dealt with a good many injuries in my day and for some reason you got off lightly. I reckon they'll strap up that ankle for you—maybe put it in a plaster cast, I don't know what the current idea is—and in a couple of days, with the help of a stick, you'll be mobile.' He turned back to Reya and told her crisply, 'I suggest you pack all your gear and take it with you. The Woolpack Hotel is comfortable, and it's near the hospital. You might give me a call when you think of it and let me know what's happening.'

Listening to him dismissing her, she felt sick. She couldn't answer and she barely nodded and after a second he went away. Warren lay back on his pillow, his hands behind his head, his eyes half closed.

'No matter what that sheep farmer has to say,' he remarked, 'I'm not going to hang around in a tinpot hospital at Djilla for a few days that just might stretch out to a fortnight. I can get specialist attention in Sydney and that's where I'll go. You can drive the car, can't you?'

Reya stared at him. 'Do you mean to Sydney?'

'That's right. I'll have this foot X-rayed, and maybe put in a day at the hospital while you get the car checked over thoroughly at the garage. We'll leave the following morning.'

She bit her lip nervously. 'Very well,' she agreed after a moment. She didn't see what else she could do, but she felt far from confident at the thought of driving a thousand or so kilometres, much of it over roads that would be hardly first class. She told Warren quietly, 'I'll get you some breakfast and then I'll do the packing.'

'That's the idea,' he said approvingly, and added as she reached the door, 'As a matter of fact, it's become rather urgent for me to get to Sydney. I had an important letter from Arthur in yesterday's mail.'

She waited, but he didn't enlarge upon that, and she continued on her way. She wondered if the fact that Berry Esmond was going to Sydney had something to do with this urgency. She forgot the whole business, however, when she reached the dining room door and discovered Marlene

169

and Jackson there, his hands on her shoulders, her face raised to his. For an instant she felt numb with shock. She didn't know if they had just kissed or were just about to kiss, but the recollection of what Marlene had said last night shot through her mind warningly: 'It will be my house soon . . .'

Marlene's light blue eyes wore an expression of triumph, and Jackson dropped his arms casually and moved to draw out a chair at the table for Reya. She said stiffly, 'I'll take some breakfast to Warren before I sit down.'

'I've asked Everlie to see to that,' he said firmly, and defeated, she took her place. Milton had already left the house, but Jackson was apparently leaving later. No doubt, she thought bitterly, he wanted to see her off the premises. She told him as she ate without appetite the chops and eggs that the housegirl had set before her, 'I shan't need to phone you about our plans after all. I can tell you now what we've decided. We're going to leave Djilla tomorrow morning.'

Marlene looked maliciously complacent, but the blue of Jackson's eyes seemed to intensify as he gazed at her.

'Just how are you going to manage that?'

She shrugged. 'I shall drive the car. Warren prefers to see a specialist in Sydney as soon as he can rather than stay in Djilla. He intends to have the X-ray first,' she finished almost defiantly.

He said nothing, but his mouth was set in an angry line. Reya looked away from him, finished her breakfast, and went to her room to pack.

She had been there for several minutes when Jackson came in. He didn't bother to knock, and seeing him standing inside the doorway, she felt almost frightened; he was so dark-faced and impassive, his curling hair was dishevelled and his blue eyes were intent. She said in a voice that shook, 'What's the matter? Why are you looking at me like that?'

'You are not to drive to Sydney,' he rapped out. 'You haven't had enough experience to take a car all that way

170

with a partly incapacitated man on your hands into the bargain. You are not to do it. Do you hear me?'

'Yes, I hear you.' Her face was white, then colour rushed into it. 'But you can't stop me. It's ridiculous for you to try to order me about. Warren and I know what we're doing.' She turned her back and Jackson stepped forward and seized her by the arm, twisting her round to face him. His blue eyes blazed and his mouth was set in a threatening line. He said tightly, 'If I wasn't so damned busy here I'd take the time off and drive you myself.'

'That would be pointless,' she said coldly, though her blood was racing. 'I can manage perfectly well. Besides, it's important to Warren that we leave tomorrow. You can forget us and carry on as usual. We shan't—we shan't be seeing you any more.' She flicked her lashes down and saw that his fists were clenched.

'You are my responsibility,' he bit out.

'I'm Warren's responsibility,' she retorted.

'You mean that?' He looked and sounded incredulous.

Something inside her screamed out, 'Of course I mean it! What do you expect? You work things so I have to go— you let me know you don't want me here, you underline it on every possible occasion—and then you protest conscience—caring. You have no more concern for me than your damned casual country has for who comes and who goes, who lives and who dies.' Of course she didn't say any that. She said a tight and tense, 'Yes,' then wrenched her arm free of him and crossed the room to the opened wardrobe and busied herself there.

After a moment she heard the bedroom door click shut and the sound of his boots as he left the house. Without even saying goodbye.

She began automatically and mindlessly to gather her things together. A little later she saw Marlene cross the garden, then there was the sound of the utility as they drove away together. Reya thought bitterly and possibly unfairly that nobody really cared what happened to people like herself and Warren. Even if Warren had been quite badly injured—even if it had been herself who had been thrown by a horse—Jackson Brand wouldn't *really* care. His attitude was that people in the outback had to be tough if they were to stay. And if you finished up with a permanent limp—like Spence over at Coolabah Creek—then that was simply what the outback handed out to you, and you accepted it and carried on. She and Warren —they shouldn't have stayed even as long as they had. In fact, they should never have come.

Tears blinded her as she flung the last of her things into her suitcase and closed it down. He was right about himself. He was tough and brutal and ugly and *utterly* impossible to live with, and he had walked out on her.

And if she was being unfair and illogical and hopelessly feminine, then she didn't care. She wanted to cry and cry.

Instead, she wiped her eyes and looked at herself without a great deal of liking in the mirror, and told herself that she would be very glad to go away and forget Jackson Brand and the outback. Without even a pleasant goodbye to remember, it was going to be just that little bit easier to erase his memory.

In his room, she found Warren already dressed, his hair groomed, one shoe on. He was sitting on the side of his bed smoking, and this morning the scent of cloves made her sick.

She packed up for him as quickly as she could.

Everlie and the two housegirls were the only people around as they left the homestead, and Warren limped down the steps and across the garden, a giggling housegirl on either side of him, Reya and Everlie with the luggage bringing up the rear. He settled himself in the back of the car while Reya, having said goodbye and thank you to Everlie, took the driver's seat. She couldn't bear to look back as she drove away, and she had to blink tears from her eyes to see where she was going.

During the drive, she concentrated entirely on the road while in the back of the car Warren appeared to be intent on his own thoughts. It was a relief not to have to talk, but

172

it needed a tremendous effort to control her own thoughts and to concentrate on making the right turnings. She certainly didn't want to finish up at Tibooburra, she reminded herself, and managed a faint smile.

At the hospital, Warren was expected, and Reya delivered him into the capable hands of a Sister and a couple of nurses.

'We shall keep Mr Livingston-Lowe here for at least one night, dear. You're his fiancée, are you?' the Sister asked.

Reya ignored the question and merely smiled and said she would be at the Woolpack Hotel if they wished to get in touch with her. It was up to Warren to let it be known that he intended to leave the following morning, and if there was any opposition, Reya was quite sure he was capable of dealing with that. She smiled wryly to herself at the critical look on his face as he looked round at what was undoubtedly a small hospital.

'I'll be in touch, Reya,' he told her, and kissed her briefly on the cheek. There was a distant look in his eyes and she thought with certainty, 'Berry Esmond means a lot more to him than I do.' If she was just the tiniest bit hurt at the realisation, it was only natural vanity, and she suspected that if she did want to opt out of taking up a career in acting it wasn't going to be at all difficult. It was just as well that Warren's enthusiasm hadn't infected her too strongly. Of course, there was the chance that Berry Esmond's arrival in Sydney was not going to make any difference to the status quo, but she somehow thought otherwise.

Presently she drove the car to the nearest garage and asked if she could have it serviced that afternoon.

'In a hurry, are you, miss?' asked the mechanic.

'I need the car in the morning,' she admitted.

'Righto, then,' he said obligingly. 'I think we can fit her in, but she won't be ready till late afternoon. That okay?'

'Fine,' said Reya, and asked him where the Woolpack Hotel was.

It was just around the corner and she went there right away, booked in, and was given a pleasant enough room that opened on to the balcony that overlooked the street. She had brought only her small overnight case with her and left the rest of her luggage in the boot of the car with one of Warren's suitcases and his camera and photographic equipment. She went downstairs to the dining room which was still open and ordered a salad and a pot of tea, though she wasn't feeling very hungry, perhaps because she was so tired. The emotional strain of the last day, plus that of driving to Djilla, had exhausted her.

Returning to her room, she threw herself on the bed and slept, despite the fact that the air was oppressively hot and still. Her dreams were troubled, and mostly concerned with the worry of driving to Sydney. It was almost a relief to be wakened by a loud knocking.

'Miss Barberton, you're wanted on the telephone!'

She struggled out of sleep, slipped on the sandals she had discarded, and went downstairs. For some reason, she thought it was going to be Jackson, to say that he would come into Djilla and drive her and Warren to Sydney. But of course it was not. It was Warren, and for several seconds she couldn't get the gist of what he was saying, confused by her dreams and her mad idea that she was about to speak to Jackson. Finally she understood that he wanted her to bring his luggage straight to the hospital.

'The car won't be ready,' she protested, bewildered.

'Take a taxi, then,' he said irritably, 'and pick up my luggage and bring it along with you. I've got a seat on this evening's plane for Sydney.'

'*One* seat?' she heard herself ask, feeling more confused than ever.

'Yes, of course.' He sounded impatient. 'You'll have to bring the car down. I don't intend to abandon it, and you're in no great hurry.'

Her heart sank. It had been bad enough to contemplate driving all that way with Warren, but the prospect of being completely on her own filled her with dread. She had a vivid mental picture of her confusion when she reached the great sprawling city of Sydney, and she knew she would be hopelessly lost and terrified. She uttered a protesting, 'But, Warren, I don't think I could——' but he cut her short.

'We'll talk in the taxi. Get a move on, will you? I've got to be out at the airfield in about a half hour.'

Feeling more than slightly panic-stricken, Reya hurried through to the reception desk to ask for a taxi to be ordered, then ran back up the stairs to fetch her handbag and tidy her hair—and to discover, as she looked through the windows across the balcony, that it was raining—and raining hard.

She did exactly as Warren asked, collected his luggage from the car that certainly wasn't yet ready, and continued in the taxi to the hospital. Warren, it appeared, was leaving with the full permission of the authorities. Rather grudgingly, he told her in the taxi, 'By a bit of good luck, your sheep farmer set the break adequately.' His ankle was in plaster, he had a handsome stick, and had apparently charmed the entire staff into understanding that he simply must get to Sydney. There were only four planes a week, and if he didn't take today's flight, then he'd be stuck here for two more days.

'But we were leaving in the morning in the car,' Reya reminded him, and he said lightly, 'Even taking the later plane would get me to Sydney faster than with you at the wheel. We'd probably have had to spend three nights on the road. You'll be all right on your own, at any rate. Just take all the time you like—I want you to promise me you won't endanger yourself by speeding, or driving when you're tired. If you think it will be a help, you can put in your last night at—well, let's say Kurrajong or Windsor, they're both pleasant places as I remember, I drove through them on the way out here. Ring me at Arthur's—I'll let you have the phone number—and I'll arrange for someone to go out and pick you up. It's only forty or fifty miles, I might even make it myself if my foot's better.'

'That's too kind of you,' she said bitterly.

He gave her a sharp look. 'What's the matter? Isn't that going to be a help?'

'A wonderful help,' she said, still bitter. Tears were stinging her eyes and she turned her face away from him and looked out at the rain that was still falling on the red earth. She said shakily, 'I'm not *really* looking forward to driving your car all that way on my own——'

'No, I'm sorry, but you'll be all right,' he said reassuringly. 'You can do it. And as I told you, I simply have to get to Sydney as soon as possible.'

'You haven't told me why,' she said, and when he was silent she asked flatly, 'Is it because Berry Esmond will be there?'

She saw she had taken him by surprise and she knew he hadn't intended telling her. 'How did you know about that?' he asked sharply.

'I had a letter from Aunt E. and she just happened to mention it—because of—because of Berenice Esmond's connection with you.'

There was a slightly longer pause, then he asked her, 'You've never been really keen on playing in *South of the Gulf*, have you?'

Reya shook her head. She felt very definitely estranged from Warren.

'I thought not. Well, I still say you could be good, but if Berry's interested, naturally I should have to prefer her. I *made* that girl, you know. Arthur wrote to me—I told you that—and it appears that she just wasn't happy in the States, which rather proves my point that she needs *me*, plus a role written with her special talents in mind. Jon wrote Marie for her, of course, then she met this other guy and thought she could do better for herself and we broke up.' He added after a moment, 'I'm not trying to drop you, Reya. Come along if you want to and we'll find you a part. But in any case you must put in an appearance in Sydney shortly—I'm quite willing to pay you well for it. Berry must be taught a lesson before I take her back.' He

176

frowned and looked out at the rain. 'You can see why I want to be there when she arrives—I can't risk having Jon or Arthur saying the wrong thing.'

Reya listened almost impersonally. Jackson was right about the selfishness and artificiality of Warren's world. Warren was more interested in his work than in human relationships, but she suspected that Berry Esmond meant more to him than any other woman. Certainly she was a great deal more important to him than was Reya Barberton. He was not at all concerned at the thought of her driving to Sydney completely alone. He thought he was dealing with her very thoughtfully in offering her an escort for the last fifty miles—and he would be totally incredulous now if she refused to have any part in this business of teaching Berry Esmond a lesson, and bringing her back to heel. Yet why should she play a part in it? She didn't, when she came to think of it, have any reason to be particularly grateful to Warren.

They had reached the airfield by now, and Warren, who took it for granted that she would comply with his wishes, occupied himself in preparing to get himself and his plaster cast out of the taxi. Then on a sudden thought he produced his wallet, and as the taxi braked, he drew out a handful of ten and twenty-dollar notes and thrust them at her.

'Here, count that, Reya, and calculate if it will pay for the car and see you through the next few days.'

'It's far too much,' she said after a swift assessment. 'There's over two hundred dollars here.'

'Keep it,' he said offhandedly. 'Give me the change in Sydney if it's on your conscience.'

The taxi driver opened the door and helped him out. From nowhere, somebody appeared to take charge of his luggage. The sun, low on the horizon, burst through the clouds and the rain stopped as if to allow Warren to board the plane in comfort. He paused to kiss Reya goodbye, to squeeze her hand to tell her she was wonderful. 'I'll ask Jon to write a special scene into *South of the Gulf* for you, darling, if that's what you'd like. Keep in touch, won't you, and I'll see you shortly in Sydney.'

She nodded hypnotically, dazed with the speed at which everything was happening. When he had gone she got back into the taxi and soon was on her way back to town, totally alone.

CHAPTER TEN

REYA didn't know when she made up her mind that she absolutely couldn't drive Warren's car to Sydney. The very thought of waking in the morning and having that ahead of her made her feel sick with nerves. She would have to find someone to come with her.

She collected the car, paid for it out of the wad of money Warren had given her, and went back to the hotel. Her room was empty and silent, and she stood looking about her feeling deserted and friendless. She needed to talk to someone—to get help . . .

The next thing she knew, she was downstairs at the telephone asking the exchange to put her through to Big Sky.

'I'm sorry, there's been a breakdown on the line due to the storm. Would you like to try again later?'

Reya said she would, and hung up, and discovered that her legs were shaking as she went back to her room. There she flung herself down on the bed and wept. She wept for herself—because she was never going to see Jackson again. She thought how she had come out to Australia all eagerness and bravado and hope—and she knew that underneath it all it had been for Jackson that she had come back. 'Jackson.' She said the name aloud on a sob. She was sure she couldn't live without him. Undoubtedly she would have to, but how hard it was going to be to forget him. She envisaged a future in which he haunted her dreams for ever. She thought again of that car and of Warren, and it seemed to her that his car meant more to Warren than she did. She didn't believe that with Berry Esmond back in his life he would have time and energy to waste trying to make a star of Reya Barberton.

Suddenly she sat up and dried her eyes and set her feet determinedly on the floor, groping for her sandals in a

179

room that had grown almost dark. There was only one thing in life that seemed important just now, and that was to see Jackson again. Just once. She would—she would throw herself on his mercy—ask for someone to go with her to Sydney; hope that by some miracle he would come. And if he sent her away, or offered to let Marlene accompany her as, with a sense of dread, she knew that he might very well do, then that would be that, she would have to take it on the chin.

'Fool!' she thought cynically as she switched on the light and hurriedly began to pack a few things she had scattered about. 'Why not accept the inevitable now?' She didn't try to answer that one. She changed into her black jeans and red cotton shirt, zipped up her overnight bag, and went downstairs to settle her hotel account.

Outside in the street was Warren's car, red and shining and handsome. Reya unlocked the door, slung in her bag, slid in behind the driving wheel, and soon was heading out of town.

She was aware of a feeling of enormous relief, as if she had escaped from a trap, and she began to feel more cheerful. The sky above was clear and starry, the rain had gone. Cool air flowed in through the window and lifted the hair lightly from the back of her neck and caressed her . . . And when at last she left the bitumen and took to the gravel, a curious sensation invaded her being. The Outback was with her, was welcoming her back. She felt herself both loved and in love, and not in the least frightened by the vast invisible emptiness all around her. There were no lights, not even a faint glimmer, not a sign that human beings had ever come to the dark, oddly beckoning outback country through which she drove. The car headlights swept occasionally over the pale trunk of a great gum tree, or brought to life stands of twisted mulgas as their shadows moved and lengthened as the car sped onwards.

And when the time came to turn off the gravel road and follow mere tracks, she swung the wheel as confidently as if some unseen spirit were guiding her.

On and on she drove, taking the turn-offs automatically, as if she had been born out here and was going home. She was bang on the dotted line all the way, almost exultantly convinced that she was doing the right thing in coming back to Jackson.

'For help, that's all,' she said aloud, reminding herself that this was merely a waking dream in which she was indulging—a dream whose ending was that Jackson took her into his arms and they lived happily ever afterwards.

Sobered, she knew that she could very well be greeted with cold indifference or even worse. He might tell her unequivocally that he was not interested in her troubles—ask her why she hadn't got her priorities right a little sooner. Very soon now, she was going to find out. She hadn't all that far to go now. As if in accord with this drop in her confidence, she began to have to fight with the steering wheel, which had suddenly developed a will of its own. Something was badly wrong, and she soon realised what it was. She was driving in deep blacksoil mud—the result of the afternoon's storm. Even as understanding reached her, the car skidded and slithered sideways alarmingly, the wheels slipped and grabbed and slipped again, and then spun round uselessly. Warren's car came to a complete though shuddering standstill angled towards the post and rail fence.

Reya sat stunned and unbelieving for a moment, feeling her face and hands clammy from that brief and losing battle with the car. She was bogged in the blacksoil. What a fool she had been! How easily she had been deluded into thinking herself the master. But the outback had tricked her and had won, and she had no idea how she was going to get the car going again.

She opened the glove box and found a torch, climbed out of the car—straight into the clinging black mud, inches deep—and took a look at the wheels. All four of them were clogged up, and she breathed deeply in an effort to subdue the tremor of fear that ran through her.

'*Think*,' she told herself. 'You're not beaten yet.'

Across the plains, an owl hooted, and she heard the howl of a dingo. She shivered involuntarily and looked around her. Wasn't the idea to get branches, strips of bark, and lay them down where the back wheels would, if you were lucky, get on to them? But suppose you took that first step, what happened next? She had a chilling fatalistic feeling that the same thing happened again. And again. *Long* stretches of the road could be impassable, Jackson had said. She looked up at the sky as if for inspiration and discovered the Southern Cross, bright and clear, tilted there. Produce the long axis to two and a half times its length, she remembered reading somewhere—in her schooldays—then drop a perpendicular and you have the south. She wanted to laugh hysterically. What was the use of that particular piece of information just now?

It was exactly then that she heard a sharp rifle shot, and her pulses leapt. Someone was out hunting the dingo she had heard howling. Almost without thought, she slipped through the wire fence and began to head roughly in the direction from which the rifle sound had come. It was hard going, and she stumbled occasionally over a tussock of stiff grass or some unevenness in the ground, but at least no more blacksoil weighted her sandals once the initial lot had fallen off. Once she saw the shadows of three big kangaroos bounding across the paddock ahead of her, and she felt strangely like a little wild animal herself as with fast-beating heart, and breath uneven, she hurried onwards. Now and again she stopped and flashed her torch around, then switched it off again, but there was no answering signal to be seen.

She had no idea how long she had been walking—miles, by the stiffness of her calf muscles!—when she reached a long stand of low dark trees that stretched away in either direction. Once through these, she told herself hopefully, she would find someone. If she didn't, she didn't know what she would do. She was by no means sure she could find her way back to the car, and she didn't relish sleeping out on the ground all night.

Making her way warily through the trees, she heard the dingo howl again—a bloodcurdling sound, uncomfortably close. Though it was, in a way, reassuring, Reya stood rigid and afraid, and the torch fell from her hands and was lost in the darkness. Her heart was beating wildly and through eyes opened wide in fright, she imagined she saw a yellow dingo slide like a shadow amongst the twisted tree trunks. After several minutes of utter and stultifying silence, she moved slowly forward. She could see through the trees now, and knew she would soon reach open ground. She could make out the vague woolly shapes of scattered sheep, and then—Her heart stood still. By a lone tree she discerned the slim dark shape of a man, and—Oh God, starlight gleamed faintly on a rifle that was levelled exactly at where she stood in the mulga scrub. Her breath caught and she held it and, afraid to move, she stayed where she was, her feet half covered by a patch of red and black flowers. She knew that if she were to move, Jackson—some sixth sense told her it was he—might fire in the belief that it was the dingo. What a melodramatic ending to her love story—to be shot by the man who had rejected her, to die here amongst the red and black flowers that waited for ever!

Her thoughts were becoming hysterical, and then nearby a pair of eyes glinted red like two spots of fire as the dingo slunk across in front of her, its yellow body momentarily touched by starlight. The next moment there was a loud explosion, and almost at her feet the creature fell to the ground, uttering a low growling sound deep in its throat.

Reya stared transfixed, almost stunned with shock. The animal shuddered and lay still. The only thing that moved was the narrow river of blood that ran slowly down across its yellow head. Then everything went dark as she collapsed into a faint . . .

When she came to consciousness, she was half lying on the ground and Jackson's arms were around her and she heard him groan softly, 'Oh, my darling, beautiful girl—what have I done to you?'

For a moment she didn't know what had happened, then memory returned and she saw again that yellow head and the blood running on to the ground, and she turned her face into his chest and felt the strong beat of his heart. Magically, her nausea went and she was conscious only of his nearness and of the happiness of coming back to him. She murmured, 'You didn't hurt me—I'm all right—it was just the—the dingo——'

'Thank God,' he said hoarsely. 'If anything had happened to you I could never have forgiven myself. When I saw you lying there—oh, God, then I knew exactly how much you mean to me, that I can't live without you.' His voice was rough with emotion, and listening, Reya thought she must be dreaming. She struggled a little against him and sat up and opened her eyes wide, and discovered they were in the open away from the trees, with the starry sky above and silence all around. Far off, yet looking almost close enough to touch, the moon had lifted itself on to the edge of the flat horizon, and its light blossomed out, yellow-gold and faintly steamy over the wet ground. It was beautiful—too beautiful to bear, too beautiful to be real.

Reya turned her head slowly to look at the man crouching beside her, the moonlight revealing the planes of his dark face and making his eyes alive and beautiful, and highlighting that black curling hair that she had longed so often to touch. Of course she was dreaming, and because of it she reached out and touched his hair and breathed out on a sigh, 'Oh, Jackson, I had to come back. Please don't send me away ever again.'

The line of his lips altered slightly and he stood up, his hand taking hold of hers to raise her beside him, and it was like being drawn gently out of a sea of soft, soft water; she seemed to feel the moonlight rush and rustle and flow around her like a soft warm wind. She felt herself lifted into the air as though she were a bird—or a flower coming into being. Jackson's arms received her and his lips were on hers, and while she knew it was a dream she knew too that it had to be true.

184

'I'll never let you go again,' he said at last, and he held her two wrists together behind her back as though she were his prisoner, and he kissed her again ...

It was not till later when they were walking to his car, that gleamed moon-speckled in the shelter of trees some distance away, that outside facts began to intrude into the world they had inhabited alone for blissful minutes, and Reya wondered half fearfully if all that had been murmured between them out there in the moonlight had vanished like a wraith.

'You haven't explained yet what happened to bring you here tonight,' he said, and though his arm was still around her, she lost some of her joyful certainty as he asked the mundane question that must of necessity bring numberless complications into their relationship

'I drove the car out from Djilla,' she began, 'but it got bogged down in the blacksoil. Then I heard the dingo—and the rifle shot—and so I started walking.'

'Livingston-Lowe's in the car?—waiting for you to come back with help?' he asked, the old familiar note of coldness in his voice.

'No,' she said at once. 'Warren left for Sydney on the plane this afternoon. He asked me to drive his car down by myself tomorrow, but I—I couldn't face it. I came here to ask you to help me—to see if someone could come with me. Marlene——' she concluded stumblingly.

He stopped walking suddenly and caught her by the shoulders, swinging her round to face him, almost fiercely. 'Is *that* why you came? Do you want to be taken back to Sydney and Livingston-Lowe and this new career of yours that hasn't yet begun—that you've wangled?' He paused and his eyes searched her face, and to her they looked like blue fire in the moonlight. 'No, Reya Barberton,' he said at last. 'I don't think that's why you're here, or that that's what you want.'

She shook her head, eyes wide, heart beating fast. 'I don't care about the acting—I never did. It was Warren's idea. It doesn't matter any more.'

'What does matter, then?'

Her lips parted. What mattered was that she should stay here at Big Sky with him, but instead of answering, she asked wildly, 'Are you going to marry Marlene?'

'Good God, no! What gave you that idea?'

She didn't tell him what Marlene had said, she told him, 'She was engaged to you before—so I thought——'

'Engaged to me before? Who on earth told you that? It's not true. Oh, I'll admit that when Jerry married again and Marlene was no longer mistress of Lilli-Pilli, she had her eye on me. Marlene's a very practical girl. But I certainly never asked her to marry me. And now—undoubtedly, Marlene will marry my jackeroo, when Jerry Ramsey makes him manager of Lilli-Pilli, which he will do. And that,' Jackson concluded firmly, 'will make a lot of people happy. So now I've answered your question, let's get back to you. If you've finished with acting—and with Warren—then what matters to you?'

'You,' she said huskily. 'Staying here. I'll—I'll help Everlie with the children, the cooking—I—I won't ask a thing of you——'

She heard his low laugh. 'Do you think either of us could go through with that? You know *exactly* what I'd ask of you if I had to see you every day.'

She felt her cheeks flare into colour. 'I wouldn't care what you asked.'

'I don't believe you would, honey.' He had been smiling, but now he sobered. 'I tried hard to teach you to hate me, but it never quite worked out that way, did it?'

Reya shook her head. 'Why did you want it to be like that?'

'Because it seemed the only way out. I fell in love with you over four years ago and I—couldn't keep my hands off you,' he said with a wry smile. 'So I just couldn't have you around. I'd promised myself years before that I'd never subject any woman to the conditions I accepted for myself —unless she'd been born to them. My own mother couldn't face up to the loneliness, the harshness, of the outback.

186

She opted out—left my father and went to the coast. E.—E. came to terms with it, but she never learned to love it. She accepted it passively after she'd made her one small moan to me, and Tom never knew. So you see, you had to go. And before you went, I'd already bruised the fragile flower of your innocence. If you stayed, it would have started an avalanche that couldn't be stopped.' He paused and looked at her almost hungrily and she began to understand what it was all about. 'You were only a kid, Reya—but I was scared of you. You were so obviously the wrong sort of girl for a tough character like me. I wanted you to hate me.'

'I thought I did,' she murmured. 'Because you sent me away. But—but I used to dream about you all the time in England. I couldn't forget you.'

'So you came back And for me, the old irresistible thing was still there, stronger than ever, and I fought against it. Hard. With occasional lapses,' he admitted with a lift of one eyebrow and a slight smile that made her pulses race.

'But you won, didn't you?' she asked, a trifle sadly. 'You sent me away again. You didn't even say goodbye.' What would have happened, she wondered, if she hadn't come back tonight? Jackson would have let her go and that would have been the end of it. The thought frightened her. It made her uncertain of herself, and it was with strange reluctance that she now let him draw her into his arms.

He didn't kiss her immediately. He said, 'Yes, I sent you away because it seemed what you wanted. I thought you wanted to become an actress—that that meant more to you than your feeling for me. That, and Warren Livingston-Lowe—you said you were his responsibility, remember? All the same, tonight while I was out here alone stalking that dingo, I got a number of things straightened out in my mind. One thing was that I loved you too much for my own comfort. When I thought that Warren Livingston-Lowe might one day make love to you, I felt sick to the very marrow of my bones. If I hadn't believed he was spending the night in hospital, I'd have got into the car and driven straight to Djilla, despite the rain and the dicey road. As it was, I cooled down and made up my mind to drive in to Djilla in the morning, as soon as it was light.'

'To—to take us to Sydney?' she asked quaveringly.

'To bring you back here,' he said. 'Whether you wanted it or not. And to promise you—as I promise you now, on my heart—that if you can't be happy here, then we'll go somewhere else to live.'

Happiness flooded her being, and she shook her head. 'I belong *here*, Jackson. I'm one of those people who keep coming back because the outback's got into their blood.'

He laughed softly. 'You say that with such conviction I almost believe you. And I thought it was me you came back to. All the same,' he asked against her lips, 'are you going to marry me?'

'Yes!' she breathed, and he held her against him in a long kiss, and Reya knew that she had truly come home to her dreamtime at last.

YOU'LL L♥VE
Harlequin Magazine

for women who enjoy reading fascinating stories of exciting romance in exotic places

SUBSCRIBE NOW!

This is a colorful magazine especially designed and published for the readers of Harlequin novels.

Now you can receive your very own copy delivered right to your home every month throughout the year for only 75¢ an issue.

This colorful magazine is available only through Harlequin Reader Service, so enter your subscription now!

In every issue...

Here's what you'll find:

♥ a complete, full-length romantic novel...illustrated in color.

♥ exotic travel feature...an adventurous visit to a romantic faraway corner of the world.

♥ delightful recipes from around the world...to bring delectable new ideas to your table.

♥ reader's page...your chance to exchange news and views with other Harlequin readers.

♥ other features on a wide variety of interesting subjects.

Start enjoying your own copies of Harlequin magazine immediately by completing the subscription reservation form.

Not sold in stores!

Harlequin Presents...

By popular demand...

36 original novels from this series—by 3 of the world's greatest romance authors.

These back issues by Anne Hampson, Anne Mather and Violet Winspear have been out of print for some time. So don't miss out; order your copies now!

All the above titles are available at 95¢ each. Please use the attached order form to indicate your requirements.   *Offer expires May 31, 1977.*

Harlequin Reader Service
ORDER FORM

Mail coupon to:
Harlequin Reader Service,
M.P.O. Box 707,
Niagara Falls, New York 14302

Canadian Residents send to:
Harlequin Reader Service,
Stratford, Ont. N5A 6W4

Please send me by return mail the books that I have checked.
I am enclosing 95¢ for each book ordered.

Please check volumes requested:

☐ 1	☐ 11	☐ 20	☐ 29
☐ 2	☐ 12	☐ 21	☐ 30
☐ 3	☐ 13	☐ 22	☐ 31
☐ 4	☐ 14	☐ 23	☐ 32
☐ 5	☐ 15	☐ 24	☐ 33
☐ 7	☐ 16	☐ 25	☐ 34
☐ 8	☐ 17	☐ 26	☐ 35
☐ 9	☐ 18	☐ 27	☐ 36
☐ 10	☐ 19	☐ 28	☐ 37

Number of books ordered_____ @ 95¢ each = $ _____

Postage and handling = $ _____.25

TOTAL = $ _____

NAME _____
(please print)

ADDRESS _____

CITY _____

STATE/PROV._____ ZIP/POSTAL CODE_____

Offer expires December 31, 1977   ROM 2057